GANDHI QUIZ

Professor A.N. Agrawal taught economics for over forty years in Ramjas College, Delhi, before retiring. He is the author of several quiz books, and lives in Delhi.

GANDHI QUIZ

A.N. Agrawal

RUPA

Published by
Rupa Publications India Pvt. Ltd 2005
7/16, Ansari Road, Daryaganj
New Delhi 110002

Sales centres:
Allahabad Bengaluru Chennai
Hyderabad Jaipur Kathmandu
Kolkata Mumbai

ISBN: 978-81-716-7335-3

Fifth impression 2016

10 9 8 7 6 5

Contents

Preface

An attempt has been made here to capture some glimpses of the life and work of Mahatma Gandhi in the multiple-choice quiz format. The facets covered range from Gandhiji's family and personal history, South Africa phase and his role in national movement to his thought and philosophy, Gandhian literature, institutions and contemporaries. For a quiz book, the contents are fairly comprehensive, covering such main aspects where the method of quizzing can be usefully applied. At the end a photo quiz has also been added to test one's ability to recognise eminent persons and institutions connected with the life and activities of Gandhiji.

While formulating quizzes on Gandhiji, effort has been made to cover not only such aspects which are very well known, but also those which are comparatively less known. Besides enabling the readers to assess the extent and depth of their knowledge and understanding of Gandhiji, it will stimulate the desire to know more and more about Gandhiji and his plan of action. Obviously enough, the relevance of this knowledge and understanding for the present-day world is, indeed, very fresh.

The material for this quiz book has been culled from large many books, Indian and foreign, available on the subject. I am very grateful to their authors and publishers for the valuable help received.

I must thank Dr. Hari Om Varma, Mrs. Nirmal Talwar and Dr. Ashok Govil for their valuable assistance in the preparation of this book. Special thanks are due to my wife, Savitri Agrawal, for constant help and encouragement.

A.N. Agrawal

1

Family and Personal History

1. Mohandas Karamchand Gandhi was born on October 2,
   (a) 1865   (b) 1867
   (c) 1869   (d) 1871

2. At which place was Gandhiji born?
   (a) Porbandar   (b) Rajkot
   (c) Wardha   (d) Junagadh

3. Which of the following statements about Gandhi is not correct?
   (a) Gandhis were originally grocers.
   (b) For three generations, from Gandhiji's grandfather, Gandhis had been Prime Ministers in several Kathiawad States.
   (c) Gandhis belonged to the *Bania* caste.
   (d) None of the above.

4. Uttamchand Gandhi, *alias* Ila Gandhi, was Gandhiji's grandfather. He rose from the lowest rung of the ladder to be the Dewan of
   (a) Bhavnagar   (b) Porbandar
   (c) Veraval   (d) Rajkot

5. A member of the Gandhi family saluted the Nawab of Junagadh with his left hand. Asked for an explanation, he said: "The right hand is already pledged to Porbandar." Who was he?
   (a) Karamchand Gandhi (b) Maganlal Gandhi
   (c) Laxmidas Gandhi (d) Uttamchand Gandhi

6. State intrigues compelled Uttamchand Gandhi to seek refuge in
   (a) Rajkot (b) Junagadh
   (c) Porbandar (d) Bhavnagar

7. Identify the number of sons of Uttamchand Gandhi.
   (a) Three (b) Four
   (c) Five (d) Six

8. Which of the following statements in respect of Uttamchand Gandhi is not correct?
   (a) He married a second time, having lost his first wife.
   (b) He had four sons by his first wife.
   (c) He was a member of the Rajasthanik Court.
   (d) He had to leave Porbandar because of state intrigues.

9. Gandhiji's father, Karamchand Gandhi, *alias* Kaba Gandhi, was for some time Prime Minister in
   (a) Rajkot (b) Porbandar
   (c) Vankaner (d) In all the three

10. Among Uttamchand Gandhi's sons, the place of Karamchand Gandhi in seniority was
    (a) Fifth (b) Fourth
    (c) Third (d) Second

11. Putlibai was the fourth and last wife of Karamchand Gandhi. Identify the number of children that she bore him.
    (a) Two
    (b) Three
    (c) Four
    (d) Five

12. How old was Karamchand Gandhi when he married Putlibai?
    (a) 34 years
    (b) 36 years
    (c) 38 years
    (d) 40 years

13. What was the age of Putlibai when she got married to Karamchand Gandhi?
    (a) 17 years
    (b) 15 years
    (c) 13 years
    (d) 12 years

14. Identify the youngest child of Putlibai.
    (a) Mohandas
    (b) Raliatbehn
    (c) Laxmidas
    (d) Karsandas

15. Which of the following statements about the Gandhi family is not correct?
    (a) Members of the Gandhi family had long ago abandoned their traditional caste occupation of trade and taken to administrative service.
    (b) Karamchand Gandhi was a member of the Rajasthanik Court.
    (c) Tulsidas was the eldest son of Uttamchand Gandhi.
    (d) Karamchand Gandhi had two daughters from his first and second marriages.

16. Karamchand Gandhi became the Dewan of Porbandar at the age of

(a) Twenty-five   (b) Twenty-eight
(c) Thirty   (d) Thirty-three

17. For nearly how many years Karamchand Gandhi served as Prime Minister in various Kathiawad States?
    (a) Twenty   (b) Twenty-four
    (c) Twenty-seven   (d) Thirty

18. Who was Gandhiji's eldest brother?
    (a) Karsandas   (b) Laxmidas
    (c) Tulsidas   (d) Maganlal

19. Of which State was Gandhiji's father a pensioner when he died?
    (a) Porbandar   (b) Vankaner
    (c) Rajkot   (d) Junagadh

20. Which of the following statements about Karamchand Gandhi is incorrect?
    (a) He had no ambition to accumulate riches and left very little property.
    (b) He had read only upto the fifth Gujarati standard.
    (c) He was a lover of his class and truthful.
    (d) He was very sweet-tempered.

21. Gandhiji was about 17 years old when he lost his
    (a) Grandfather   (b) Father
    (c) Mother   (d) Uncle

22. Approximately how old was Gandhiji when his father left Porbandar service and moved with family to Rajkot?

(a) Five years   (b) Seven years
(c) Nine years   (d) Ten years

23. Which of the following games/exercises did Gandhiji like most during his student days?
(a) Long walk   (b) Football
(c) Gymnastics   (d) Hockey

24. Gandhiji entered Alfred High School at Rajkot in
(a) 1883   (b) 1882
(c) 1881   (d) 1880

25. When did Gandhiji pass the Matriculation Examination?
(a) 1885   (b) 1886
(c) 1887   (d) 1888

26. After matriculation Gandhiji joined the Samaldas College at Bhavnagar, but he left it and returned home at the end of
(a) One month   (b) Two months
(c) First term   (d) Second term

27. What was Gandhiji's age when he got married to Kasturbai?
(a) 16 years   (b) 15 years
(c) 14 years   (d) 13 years

28. Where did Gandhiji's marriage with Kasturbai take place?
(a) Porbandar   (b) Rajkot
(c) Junagadh   (d) Jamnagar

29. Identify the friend who led Gandhiji astray to meat-eating for a while.

(a) Sheik Mehtab   (b) Abdul Karim
(c) Yusuf Ismail   (d) Aslam Khan

30. During his childhood Gandhiji had in him a fear of ghosts and spirits. Who suggested to him the repetition of *Ramanama* as a remedy for this fear?
    (a) Lodha Maharaj
    (b) His mother
    (c) Family priest
    (d) Rambha, an old servant of the family

31. Which of the following plays left a deep impression on Gandhiji?
    (a) *Harishchandra*   (b) *Shravana Kumar*
    (c) Both (a) and (b)   (d) *Shakuntala*

32. Identify the statement which is not correct.
    (a) Kasturbai had never been to any school.
    (b) Kasturbai's father, Gokuldas Makanji, was a state official.
    (c) Gandhiji and Kasturbai were of about the same age.
    (d) None of the above.

33. Gandhiji confessed his guilt of stealing for the purpose of smoking in a letter, promising never to steal in future and asking for adequate punishment. To whom was this letter addressed?
    (a) Father   (b) Uncle
    (c) Mother   (d) Eldest brother

34. Who suggested and goaded the Gandhian family to send Gandhiji to England to study Law?

(a) Kevalram
(b) Mavji Dave
(c) Virchand Gandhi
(d) Krishna Shankar Pandya

35. The money needed for Gandhiji's journey and for his expenses in England were raised through
    (a) State help   (b) Bank credit
    (c) Sale of ornaments (d) Loan from a friend

36. While leaving for England, Gandhiji carried with him a letter of introduction for
    (a) Dalpatram Shukla   (b) P.J. Mehta
    (c) Dadabhai Naoroji   (d) All of them

37. On his voyage to London Gandhiji had the benefit of the company of Tryambakrai Mazumdar, an experienced man of mature age. What was his profession?
    (a) Doctor   (b) Lawyer
    (c) Businessman   (d) State official

38. About how old was Gandhiji when he reached London to become a barrister?
    (a) 17 years   (b) 19 years
    (c) 20 years   (d) 21 years

39. Who came to see Gandhiji on the day of his arrival in London at the Victoria Hotel and gave him the first lesson in English etiquette?
    (a) Prince Ranjitsinhji (b) Kevalram
    (c) P.J. Mehta   (d) None of the above

40. Before starting his regular law study in London, Gandhiji devoted some time every day to the reading of

(a) *Daily Telegraph*　　(b) *Pall Mall Gazette*
(c) *Daily News*　　　　(d) All the three

41. Gandhiji passed the London Matric in 1890 in the month of
    (a) February　　(b) April
    (c) June　　　　(d) October

42. Who of the following attempted to bring Gandhiji over to the Christian faith during his stay in London?
    (a) Charles Bradlaugh　　(b) Josiah Oldfield
    (c) Parker　　　　　　　(d) Edwin Arnold

43. In the company of two theosophists, Gandhiji read the *Gita* for the first line in London towards the
    (a) Beginning of 1890　　(b) Close of 1890
    (c) Beginning of 1889　　(d) Close of 1889

44. About a book on vegetarianism, Gandhiji made the following observation:
    "I read the book from cover to cover and was very much impressed by it. From the date of reading this book, I may claim to have become a vegetarian by choice. I blessed the day on which I had taken the vow before my mother".
    Identify the book.
    (a) Salt's *Plea for Vegetarianism*
    (b) William's *The Ethics of Diet*
    (c) Kingsford's *The Perfect Way in Diet*
    (d) None of the above

45. How many months of hard labour were devoted by Gandhiji to read Broom's *Common Law* which he described as "a big but interesting Volume"?

(a) Eleven   (b) Nine

(c) Seven   (d) Six

46. To become a barrister in England, one had to join one of the Inns of Court. After obtaining admission, Gandhiji joined the Inner Temple on
    (a) September 4, 1888   (b) October 27, 1888
    (c) November 6, 1888   (d) November 21, 1888

47. Which of the following statements about Gandhiji, as a student in London, is not correct?
    (a) In his second attempt he chose Light and Heat instead of Chemistry for the London Matriculation.
    (b) His young mind tried to unify the teachings of the *Gita*, the *Light of Asia* and the *Sermon on the Mount*.
    (c) On the suggestion of a Christian friend, he read the Bible. He was greatly impressed by the *Old Testament* which he compared with the *Gita*.
    (d) None of the above.

48. During his stay in London, Gandhiji chiefly moved among
    (a) Reformers   (b) Clergymen
    (c) Vegetarians   (d) All of them

49. Reading of a particular book, while as a student in London, disabused Gandhiji of the notion fostered by the missionaries that Hinduism was rife with superstition and stimulated in him the desire to read books on Hinduism. Identify the book.

9

(a) *Key to Theosophy*
(b) *Heroes and Hero-Worship*
(c) *Light of Asia*
(d) None of these

50. When was Gandhiji called to the Bar, thus becoming a full-fledged barrister?
(a) July 28, 1891 (b) July 10, 1891
(c) June 10, 1891 (d) May 15, 1891

51. As advised by friends, Gandhiji went to Bombay to establish practice, gain experience of the High Court and study Indian Law. But he failed to get enough work over there, and therefore left Bombay for Rajkot within
(a) Three months (b) Six months
(c) Nine months (d) One year

52. After leaving Bombay, Gandhiji came to Rajkot where he set up his own office. Here his main work was to draft applications and memorials which enabled him, on a monthly average, to get about
(a) Rs. 800 (b) Rs. 700
(c) Rs. 500 (d) Rs. 300

53. How many children did Gandhiji have?
(a) Six (b) Five
(c) Four (d) Three

54. When was Gandhiji's last child born?
(a) 1900 (b) 1898
(c) 1897 (d) 1896

55. Who was the eldest son of Gandhiji?
    (a) Harilal   (b) Ramdas
    (c) Devdas   (d) Manilal

56. Devdas was Gandhiji's
    (a) Eldest child   (b) Second child
    (c) Third child   (d) Youngest child

57. When did Gandhiji take the vow of *brahmacharya* or celebacy for life?
    (a) 1904   (b) 1906
    (c) 1908   (d) 1910

58. Who of the following sons of Gandhiji was brought up exclusively by him under his care?
    (a) Manilal   (b) Ramdas
    (c) Devdas   (d) Both (b) & (c)

59. Identify the sister of Gandhiji.
    (a) Gangabehn   (b) Raliatbehn
    (c) Danibehn   (d) Mirabehn

60. How old was Gandhiji when he made the first public speech in his life?
    (a) 29 years   (b) 27 years
    (c) 25 years   (d) 23 years

61. Gandhiji's son, Harilal, accepted Islam in May 1936 in the midst of a large congregation in a mosque in
    (a) Ahmedabad   (b) Jamnagar
    (c) Rajkot   (d) Bombay

62. Maganlal Gandhi, a grandson of one of Gandhiji's uncles, had been with Gandhiji in his work since
    (a) 1915   (b) 1910
    (c) 1904   (d) 1902

63. Identify the member of the Gandhi family who devoted his life to South Africa to carry on Gandhiji's work.
    (a) Maganlal Gandhi   (b) Manilal Gandhi
    (c) Devdas Gandhi   (d) Kanu Gandhi

64. When Gandhiji wrote to his elder brother, Laxmidas, declaring his disinterestedness in worldly possessions?
    (a) 1906   (b) 1908
    (c) 1910   (d) 1912

65. At which place Gandhiji took the momentous decision to don a lion cloth?
    (a) Wardha   (b) Ahmedabad
    (c) Varanasi   (d) Madurai

66. Identify the grand-daughter of Gandhiji who is settled in South Africa
    (a) Abha Gandhi   (b) Tara Bhattacharjee
    (c) Ela Ramgobin   (d) None of the above

67. When Gandhiji got his head shaved, discarded his clothes and settled for a lion cloth?
    (a) 1920   (b) 1921
    (c) 1923   (d) 1925

68. Who was the resident medical attendant to Gandhiji at his Sabarmati Ashram?
    (a) Sucheta Kripalani   (b) P.J. Mehta
    (c) Sushila Nayar   (d) Pyarelal

69. How old was Gandhiji when he first wrote a number of articles on vegetarianism in an English magazine, *The Vegetarian*?

(a) 21 years   (b) 22 years
(c) 23 years   (d) 24 years

70. Who worked as Private Secretary to Mahatma Gandhi?
    (a) Vinoba Bhave   (b) Mahadev Desai
    (c) J.B. Kripalani   (d) Kaka Kalelkar

71. On which day in June 1915 was the *Kaiser-i-Hind* Gold Medal conferred on Gandhiji for his public services?
    (a) 22nd   (b) 15th
    (c) 10th   (d) 3rd

72. Gandhiji had the first experience of jail life in
    (a) 1906   (b) 1908
    (c) 1910   (d) 1912

73. How many times was Gandhiji jailed?
    (a) Eleven   (b) Nine
    (c) Eight   (d) Seven

74. Approximately how old was Gandhiji when he came out of the prison gates for the last time?
    (a) 65 years   (b) 69 years
    (c) 71 years   (d) 75 years

75. Identify the place where Gandhiji served his last jail sentence.
    (a) Wardha   (b) Pune
    (c) Ahmedabad   (d) Bombay

76. The first jail sentence awarded to Gandhiji in India by the British Government was for a period of
    (a) One year   (b) Two years
    (c) Four years   (d) Six years

77. In all about how many months did Gandhiji spend in jail during his life time?
   (a) 60   (b) 72
   (c) 82   (d) 90

75. When in 1944 was Gandhiji released unconditionally from detention for the last time?
   (a) May 6   (b) April 10
   (c) March 25   (d) February 15

79. During his last imprisonment Gandhiji devoted the bulk of his time to writing and serious reading. Besides religious literature, books on which of the following subjects were chiefly studied by him?
   (a) Anatomy   (b) Grammar
   (c) Economics   (d) All of these

80. Gandhiji read the Volume I of Karl Marx's *Das Capital* in the Aga Khan Palace for the first time at the age of about
   (a) 74 years   (b) 70 years
   (c) 68 years   (d) 65 years

81. Kasturbai Gandhi died in detention at
   (a) Yeravda Jail   (b) Aga Khan Palace
   (c) Wardha Jail   (d) Ahmednagar Fort

82. Identify the member of the Gandhi family who nursed Kasturbai during her last days of illness.
   (a) Kanu Gandhi   (b) Devdas Gandhi
   (c) Raliatbehn   (d) Manilal Gandhi

83. How old was Kasturbai Gandhi at the time of her death?

(a) 70 years   (b) 72 years
(c) 74 years   (d) 76 years

84. Gandhiji had the company of Kasturbai for about
   (a) 58 years   (b) 60 years
   (c) 62 years   (d) 65 years

85. Where lies the Samadhi of Kasturbai Gandhi?
   (a) Wardha   (b) Porbandar
   (c) Ahmedabad   (d) Pune

86. Gandhiji, the votary of non-violence was shot dead on January 30, 1948 at Birla House, New Delhi, shortly after 5 P.M while going to the prayer meeting. Which was that fateful day of the week?
   (a) Monday   (b) Wednesday
   (c) Friday   (d) Saturday

87. Few days before Gandhiji's assassination a bomb was thrown at Gandhiji's prayer meeting, but no one was injured. Only a portion of the boundary wall of Birla House was damaged. Who had thrown the bomb?
   (a) Madan Lal   (b) Nathu Ram Godse
   (c) Vinayak Ram Godse   (d) Sohan Lal

88. The assassin of Gandhiji was a journalist from
   (a) Bombay   (b) Pune
   (c) Bhopal   (d) Nagpur

89. The body of Gandhiji was carried on a made-over army weapon-carrier. How many men of the army, navy and air force pulled it by ropes?
   (a) 200   (b) 175
   (c) 150   (d) 100

90. About how many lakh persons marched as part of Gandhiji's funeral procession?
    (a) Eight   (b) Ten
    (c) Twelve   (d) Fifteen

91. Who urged that the body of Gandhiji be preserved like Lenin's body in Moscow?
    (a) Lord Wavell   (b) C.F. Andrews
    (c) Lord Mountbatten (d) Mikhail Sholokhov

92. Very few persons in recorded history received such spontaneous tributes of universal praise, reverence and love as did Mahatma Gandhi at his death. Around how many condolence messages were received by the Indian Government from foreign countries alone?
    (a) 3000   (b) 2500
    (c) 2200   (d) 2000

93. Besides being Gandhiji's death anniversary, 30th January in the country is also observed as a
    (a) Martyrdom Day   (b) Anti-Leprosy Day
    (c) Women's Day   (d) Both (a) and (b)

94. Who of the following members of the Gandhi family looked after the Phoenix Settlement of South Africa and its activities after Gandhiji's return from that country?
    (a) Manilal Gandhi   (b) Sushilabehn Gandhi
    (c) Arun Gandhi   (d) All of them

95. In how many countries of the world was the birth centenary year of Gandhiji celebrated?
    (a) 92   (b) 84
    (c) 75   (d) 70

96. Who of the following Gandhis was actively associated with the work of preparing documentaries on Gandhiji's life for exhibition in India and abroad undertaken by the Gandhi Films Committee?
   (a) Rajmohan Gandhi   (b) Devdas Gandhi
   (c) Arun Gandhi   (d) Manilal Gandhi

2

South Africa Phase

1. A well-known firm of Porbandar, Dada Abdulla & Co., engaged the services of Gandhiji in a law suit pending in a South African Court, involving a large sum of
   - (a) £ 30,000
   - (b) £ 40,000
   - (c) £ 50,000
   - (d) £ 60,000

2. Besides first class return fare and meeting all expenses during the period of stay in South Africa, Dada Abdulla & Co. agreed to pay to Gandhiji a fee of
   - (a) £ 105
   - (b) £ 150
   - (c) £ 205
   - (d) £ 250

3. Identify the period for which the services of Gandhiji were secured by Dada Abdulla & Co.
   - (a) Three months
   - (b) Six months
   - (c) Nine months
   - (d) One year

4. At which place in South Africa was Gandhiji received by Abdulla Sheth, his first client in that country?

(a) Pretoria   (b) Charlestown
(c) Durban   (d) Johannesburg

5. At the time of Gandhiji's visit to South Africa, the country consisted of four units. Which of the four units bore a distinctly English imprint?
   (a) The Cape Colony
   (b) The Orange Free State
   (c) Natal
   (d) The Transvaal

6. When Gandhiji went to South Africa, the number of Indian emigrants settled over there was around
   (a) 100,000   (b) 125,000
   (c) 150,000   (d) 180,000

7. The first batch of indentured labourers from India reached South Africa on November 16,
   (a) 1850   (b) 1860
   (c) 1870   (d) 1880

8. In which South African unit had most of the Indian emigrants taken up abode?
   (a) The Transvaal
   (b) Natal
   (c) The Cape Colony
   (d) The Orange Free State

9. The Indian labourers under the indenture system initially came to South Africa for a period of
   (a) Ten years   (b) Seven years
   (c) Five years   (d) Three years

10. The indentured and ex-indentured Indian labourers hailed mainly from

(a) Bihar   (b) Uttar Pradesh
(c) Tamil Nadu   (d) Both (b) & (c)

11. The Indians first entered the Transvaal in
    (a) 1881   (b) 1875
    (c) 1873   (d) 1870

12. The District Magistrate of which place asked Gandhiji to take off his turban in the court which he refused and left the court promptly?
    (a) Pretoria   (b) Durban
    (c) Johannesburg   (d) Maritzburg

13. In which area of South Africa was the anti-Indian feeling comparatively less intense when Gandhiji arrived in that country?
    (a) The Cape Colony
    (b) Natal
    (c) The Transvaal
    (d) The Orange Free State

14. Identify the incorrect statement.
    (a) By 1893 Indians had been hounded out of the Orange Free State.
    (b) The firm of Dada Abdulla carried on trade in Durban.
    (c) Dada Abdulla's rival firm traded in Pretoria under the designation of Taib Haji Khanmamad.
    (d) None of the above.

15. At which place in South Africa was the case of Dada Abdulla & Co. pending in the court for which Gandhiji was engaged?
    (a) Durban   (b) Pretoria
    (c) Johannesburg   (d) Maritzburg

16. While holding a first-class ticket Gandhiji was ordered by a railway official to shift to the van compartment. On his refusal to comply with the unjust order, a constable was called to push him out bag and baggage. Identify the railway station where this incident took place.
    (a) Pretoria   (b) Standerton
    (c) Maritzburg   (d) Charlestown

17. Who of the following desired to convert Gandhiji to Christianity in South Africa?
    (a) A.W. Baker   (b) Mrs MacDonald
    (c) William Godfrey   (d) Spencer Walton

18. The European planters of Natal were very much against the stay of ex-indentured labourers, living as free Indians in Natal. What was approximately the number of ex-indentured labourers and free Indians over there?
    (a) 10,000   (b) 15,000
    (c) 20,000   (d) 30,000

19. In the Orange Free State the Indians were deprived of all their rights by a special law enacted in
    (a) 1876   (b) 1880
    (c) 1884   (d) 1888

20. A stringent enactment was passed in the Transvaal in 1885 which was amended next year in 1886, requiring all Indians to pay poll tax as fee for their entry into the Transvaal. What was the amount of the poll tax?
    (a) £ 1   (b) £ 2
    (c) £ 3   (d) £ 5

21. The Natal Law Society opposed Gandhiji's application for admission as an advocate of the Supreme Court of Natal on the ground that the law did not contemplate that coloured barristers should be placed on the roll. The Supreme Court, however, over-ruled the Law Society's objection and granted his application. This brought Gandhiji into further prominence. Who had advocated his cause?
    (a) W.P. Schreiner   (b) John Molteno
    (c) Harry Escombe   (d) Merriman

22. To organise Indians and enable them to lead an honourable life Gandhiji founded the Natal Indian Congress which came into being on
    (a) June 7, 1894   (b) July 15, 1894
    (c) August 10, 1894   (d) August 22, 1894

23. To which of the following offices of the Natal Indian Congress was Gandhiji appointed for the first year of its establishment?
    (a) President
    (b) Vice-President
    (c) Hon. Secretary
    (d) Chairman of the Working Committee

24. Unlike the Indian National Congress, the Natal Congress held regular meetings of its members. What was the minimum member of meetings that was prescribed to be held in a year?
    (a) Three   (b) Six
    (c) Ten   (d) Twelve

25. Though endeavours were made on behalf of the Natal Indian Congress to obtain the maximum amount from each member and quite many paid

twenty-four pounds a year, a certain minimum amount of annual fee for membership of the Congress was prescribed. What was this minimum amount?

(a) One pound   (b) Three pounds
(c) Five pounds   (d) Seven pounds

26. Gandhiji was the first Indian to be enrolled as an Advocate of the Supreme Court of Natal in 1894 in the month of

(a) September   (b) October
(c) November   (d) December

27. The Natal Government in 1894 sought to impose an annual tax of £ 25 on the ex-indentured Indians. What was the real reason behind this move?

(a) To collect more revenues
(b) To penalise them for their anti-Government activities
(c) The white traders were nervous because of the skill, intelligence and enterprise of the Indians
(d) Both (a) and (b)

28. As time passed, Gandhiji got more and more committed to the cause of Indians in South Africa. He also came to realise that people over there felt the need of his presence. So he made up his mind to go home, fetch his wife and children and then return and settle over there. With the leave of the community he left for India in 1896 for a period of

(a) Three months   (b) Six months
(c) Eight months   (d) One year

29. On June 5, 1896 Gandhiji sailed for India to fetch his wife and children as also to do some public work

by educating public opinion and creating more interest in the Indians in South Africa. During the voyage he began learning

(a) Tamil   (b) Urdu
(c) Both (a) and (b)   (d) Bengali

30. Soon after reaching India Gandhiji began writing a pamphlet *The Grievances of the British Indians in South Africa* which came to be known afterwards as the *Green Pamphlet* because of its green cover. Where did Gandhiji write this pamphlet?

(a) Ahmedabad   (b) Bombay
(c) Allahabad   (d) Rajkot

31. The copies of *Green Pamphlet*, written by Gandhiji and published on August 14, 1896 were dispatched to all the papers and leaders of every party in India. How many copies of this pamphlet were printed?

(a) Ten thousand   (b) Five thousand
(c) Three thousand   (d) One thousand

32. Besides the circulation of the *Green Pamphlet,* Gandhiji also tried to educate public opinion in cities on the South African question by organising meetings. Identify the first city that Gandhiji chose for this purpose.

(a) Calcutta   (b) Delhi
(c) Bombay   (d) Madras

33. As a result of intensive public activities of Gandhiji, people in the country came to know of the various disabilities of the Indian settlers in South Africa. When did the Indian National Congress pass the first resolution on South Africa?

(a) 1894   (b) 1896
(c) 1897   (d) 1898

34. At which place in India Gandhiji had the most en-
thusiastic audience in support of the South African
movement?
   (a) Ahmedabad   (b) Surat
   (c) Calcutta   (d) Madras

35. The editor of which paper placed his office and jour-
nal at the disposal of Gandhiji and even allowed him
to make any changes he liked in the editorial on
South Africa?
   (a) *The Statesman*
   (b) *The Englishman*
   (c) *The Pioneer*
   (d) *The Amrit Bazar Patrika*

36. Identify the place where Gandhiji received an urgent
cable from Natal requesting him to return at once.
   (a) Delhi   (b) Madras
   (c) Calcutta   (d) Bombay

37. Gandhiji set sail by S.S. *Courland*, a second time for
South Africa, with Kasturbai and their two sons,
along with the only son of his widowed sister on
   (a) November 18, 1896   (b) November 30, 1896
   (c) December 10, 1896   (d) December 20, 1896

38. On his landing at Durban, Gandhiji was assaulted by
a furious white mob and would have been lynched
but for the timely police protection. With bruises all
over his body, Gandhiji was escorted by the police to
a friend's house. Identify the friend.

(a) Parsec Rustonga   (b) Abdulla Sheth
(c) Abdul Kadir   (d) Ramsamy Naidoo

39. Which of the following statements in respect of Gandhiji's second visit to South Africa is incorrect?
    (a) Dada Abdulla offered to take Gandhiji and his family on his newly acquired steam ship, *Courland*, free of charge, which he gratefully declined.
    (b) Kasturbai Gandhi and children adopted the Parsi style of dress on their first voyage.
    (c) The steamer, *Courland*, cast anchor in the port of Durban on December 18, 1896.
    (d) None of the above.

40. The friend's house, where Gandhiji was taken for shelter under police protection was surrounded by white hoodlums, yelling for him. With the approach of night as the yelling crowd increased and shouting got intensified, a message was sent to Gandhiji to wear a disguise and leave in order to save his family and his friend from harm. Gandhiji accepted the advice and escaped from the house in disguise. Who had sent this message to Gandhiji?
    (a) F.A. Laughton   (b) H. sparks
    (c) Alexander   (d) Harry Escombe

41. Accompanied by two detectives in disguise, Gandhiji escaped from his friend's house disguised as a/an
    (a) Indian merchant   (b) Parsi
    (c) Madrasi labourer   (d) Indian constable

42. When Gandhiji reached South Africa for the second time, he originally intended to stay over there for

about a couple of months. But his actual stay got extended to about
(a) Five years (b) Four years
(c) Three years (d) Two years

43. Which of the following statements is not correct?
   (a) Two sons of Gandhiji were born in India.
   (b) In Durban Gandhiji had a house in a pleasant suburb which was suitably furnished. He had a servant and a cook.
   (c) Gandhiji engaged an English governess at £ 7 a month to impart some regular instruction to his children.
   (d) None of the above.

44. Although Gandhiji's sympathies were all with the Boers, his loyalty to the British Empire led him to side with the British when the Boer War broke out in 1899 in the month of
   (a) June (b) August
   (c) October (d) December

45. Gandhiji helped the British during the Boer War by organising the Indian Ambulance Corps. For its formation he collected together a corps of 1,100 volunteers. About how many of them were free Indians?
   (a) 200 (b) 300
   (c) 400 (d) 500

46. The Indian Ambulance Corps, formed by Gandhiji, did splendid work and its services were highly lauded by the British papers. After how many months of its formation was it disbanded?
   (a) Two (b) Four
   (c) Six (d) Eight

47. Which of the following statements in respect of the Indian Ambulance Corps is incorrect?
    (a) Gandhiji organised it with nearly forty leaders.
    (b) Its rank and file received the ordinary bearers pay.
    (c) The leaders gave their services free.
    (d) None of the above.

48. Taking leave of Natal Indians, Gandhiji with his family left for India for the second time towards the
    (a) Beginning of 1900   (b) Middle of 1900
    (c) Close of 1900   (d) Close of 1901

49. On reaching India from South Africa for the second time, identify the place where Gandhiji decided to settle down to practise Law as also do public work.
    (a) Bombay   (b) Rajkot
    (c) Ahmedabad   (d) Jamnagar

50. On his third visit to South Africa Gandhiji was accompanied by
    (a) Kasturbai Gandhi and children
    (b) Maganlal Gandhi
    (c) Three or four enterprising youths who were ready to leave the trodden path and venture abroad
    (d) Both (b) and (c)

51. In which year was Gandhiji enrolled as Attorney of the Supreme Court of Transvaal?
    (a) 1904   (b) 1903
    (c) 1902   (d) 1901

52. Having got himself enrolled as a duly qualified attorney of the Transvaal Supreme Court, Gandhiji set

up his office in the legal quarters of Johannesburg. Soon his legal work multiplied and he could not cope with it single-handed. Whom he invited to join him in his fast increasing work?

(a) Polak   (b) Ritch

(c) Both (a) and (b)   (d) Godfrey

53. The walls of Gandhiji's office at Johannesburg were adorned with four pictures. Three walls bore the pictures of Ranade, Mrs Beasant and W.W. Hunter. The fourth wall had the picture of

(a) Lord Christ   (b) Lord Krishna

(c) His father   (d) Dadabhai Naoroji

54. Gandhiji founded the Transvaal British Indian Association in

(a) 1902   (b) 1903

(c) 1904   (d) 1905

55. The Transvaal British Indian Association was formed to win justice and citizenship for Indians. Until his final return to India, Gandhiji was the

(a) President

(b) Honorary Secretary

(c) Legal adviser

(d) Both (b) and (c)

56. Identify the incorrect statement.

(a) During his first sojourn in South Africa, Gandhiji had been under the influence of theosophists.

(b) Gandhiji on his arrival in South Africa for the third time secured permit for entry in the Transvaal through the good offices of Alexander.

    (c) Despite holding proper permit, Gandhiji's name was omitted from the deputation list by the Asiatic Department.

    (d) None of the above.

57. Who in South Africa gave Gandhiji *Unto This Last* to read which proved to be one of the most decisive books of his life?

    (a) Albert West   (b) H.S.L. Polak

    (c) Parsee Rustomji   (d) Mansukhlal Nazar

58. Which of the following teachings of *Unto This Last* had never occurred to him prior to its reading?

    (a) That the good of the individual is contained in the good of all.

    (b) That a lawyer's work has the same value as the barber's as all have the same right of earning their livelihood from their work.

    (c) That the life of the tiller of the soil and the handicraftsman is the life worth living.

    (d) Both (a) and (b)

59. To put the ideas of *Unto This Last* into practice, Gandhiji founded the Phoenix Settlement near Durban which came into being in the middle of the year

    (a) 1902   (b) 1904

    (c) 1906   (d) 1908

60. What sum was laid down as the monthly allowance per head, irrespective of colour or nationality, for the members of the Phoenix Settlement?

    (a) £ 3   (b) £ 5

    (c) £ 7   (d) £ 10

61. Excluding the paid workers, the settlers of Phoenix were required to make a living by manual labour. How much land was given to each settler?
    (a) One acre   (b) Two acres
    (c) Three acres   (d) Four acres

62. On the pattern of phoenix Settlement, Gandhiji started another cooperative venture, known as Tolstoy Farm, near
    (a) Johannesburg   (b) Charlestown
    (c) Natal   (d) Pretoria

63. The Tolstoy Farm was used as a home for passive resisters and their indigent families. Who provided the land for it free of any rent or charge?
    (a) Abdulla Hajee Adam
    (b) Parsee Rustomjee
    (c) Hermann Kallenback
    (d) H.S.L. Polak

64. In which month of 1910 did the first batch of *satya-grahis* come to work and live on the Tolstoy Farm?
    (a) March   (b) June
    (c) September   (d) November

65. Which of the following statements in respect of the Tolstoy Farm is incorrect?
    (a) It was a smaller place than the Phoenix Settle-ment.
    (b) The building work was planned by H. Kallenbach.
    (c) The men's quarters were separate from the women's.
    (d) There was no cot on the farm and all slept on the floor.

66. To bring the Europeans and Indians closer together, to educate the public opinion as also to show the people their duties and rights, Gandhiji launched the weekly, *Indian Opinion.* in South Africa from
(a) Phoenix
(b) Johannesburg
(c) Charlestown
(d) Durban

67. As in the case of Boer War, Gandhiji again raised the Indian Ambulance Corps to render service during the Zulu 'Rebellion' which broke out in Natal in
(a) 1904
(b) 1905
(c) 1906
(d) 1908

68. With how many volunteers Gandhiji raised the Indian Ambulance Corps for the Zulu 'Rebellion'?
(a) 50
(b) 40
(c) 34
(d) 24

69. With Gandhiji holding the temporary rank of Sergent-Major, the Indian Ambulance Corps during the Zulu 'Rebellion' remained on active service for nearly
(a) Four weeks
(b) Six weeks
(c) Eight weeks
(d) Ten weeks

70. Gandhiji organised hospital during the outbreak of plague in 1904 in
(a) Johannesburg
(b) Durban
(c) Pretoria
(d) Volksrust

71. To be able to devote his maximum time to the *Satyagraha* struggle in South Africa, Gandhiji gave up his legal practice in
(a) 1911
(b) 1910
(c) 1909
(d) 1908

72. When Gandhiji stopped his legal practice, his annual earnings from the profession amounted to around
    (a) £ 3 to 4,000
    (b) £ 4 to 5,000
    (c) £ 5 to 6,000
    (d) £ 8 to 9,000

73. Most of Gandhiji's savings were devoted to public cause. The Phoenix Settlement alone cost him about
    (a) £ 7,000
    (b) £ 5,000
    (c) £ 4,000
    (d) £ 3,000

74. To protest against the anti-Indian Ordinance issued by the Transvaal Government, a mass meeting was held at Johannesburg which adopted the famous Fourth Resolution by which the Indians resolved not to submit to the Ordinance and to suffer all the penalties attaching to such non-submission. This marked the actual beginning of the *Satyagraha* campaign in South Africa under Gandhiji's leadership. Which day was it?
    (a) September 11, 1906
    (b) September 24, 1906
    (c) October 12, 1906
    (d) October 20, 1906

75. The Indian Community of the Transvaal decided to send a two-member deputation to England to explain its case in respect of the Ordinance to the Imperial Government. The deputation left for England in October, 1906. One member was Gandhiji. Who was the other member?
    (a) Abdul Gani
    (b) H.O. Ali
    (c) Abdulla Haji Adam
    (d) Parsee Rustomji

76. When was the first *hartal* organised by Gandhiji in South Africa?
    (a) September 10, 1908
    (b) August 7, 1908
    (c) July 29, 1908
    (d) July 23, 1908

77. With two breaks in between Gandhiji stayed in South Africa for about
    (a) 15 years   (b) 17 years
    (c) 19 years   (d) 21 years

78. How many times was Gandhiji arrested during the struggle period in South Africa?
    (a) Four   (b) Six
    (c) Eight   (d) Nine

79. Gandhiji was sentenced to imprisonment for the first time in South Africa on January 10, 1908 for failure to leave Transvaal. Identify the period of sentence.
    (a) Two months   (b) Four months
    (c) Six months   (d) Nine months

80. At which place in South Africa did Gandhiji suffer solitary confinement?
    (a) Johannesburg   (b) Pretoria
    (c) Both (a) and (b) (d) Volksrust

81. From the prison of which place in South Africa Gandhiji sent this message to his people: "Keep absolutely firm to the end. Suffering is our remedy. Victory is certain."
    (a) Durban   (b) Germiston
    (c) Volksrust   (d) Pietersburg

82. Gandhiji was released unconditionally from jail in South Africa in 1913 in the month of
    (a) December   (b) November
    (c) October   (d) August

83. Who of the following *satyagrahis* succumbed to jail hardships during the *satyagraha* movement launched by Gandhiji in South Africa?
    (a) Harbat Singh   (b) Valliamma
    (c) Nagappan   (d) All of them

84. As the Indian struggle in South Africa gathered momentum, the name 'Passive Resistance' was found inadequate to express its real meaning. Gandhiji offered a small prize in *Indian Opinion* for suggesting an appropriate title for the new struggle. The word *'Sadagraha'* was adjudged the best designation which was changed to *'Satyagraha'* by Gandhiji. Who made the prize-winning suggestion?
    (a) Maganlal Gandhi   (b) P.K. Naidoo
    (c) Sorabji Shapurji   (d) None of the above

85. Who was deputed by General Smuts to interview Gandhiji in prison with the terms of settlement?
    (a) William Hosken   (b) Albert Cartright
    (c) Jordan   (d) Essop Mian

86. Which of the following statements is not correct?
    (a) On two occasions in South Africa, Gandhiji was made to march from the jail to the station in prison garb, handcuffed and with his prison kit on his head.
    (b) Gandhiji served his first term of imprisonment in the Fort in Johannesburg.
    (c) Gandhiji took the oath of passive resistance against the newly promulgated Transvaal Asiatic Law Amendment Ordinance on September 11, 1906.
    (d) None of the above.

87. At which place was the first permit office opened on July 1, 1907 for the registration of Indians under the Registration Act?
    (a) Pretoria (b) Johannesburg
    (c) Pietersburg (d) Volksrust

88. On which day of February 1908 did Mir Alam and his associates mercilessly attack Gandhiji while he was going to the Registration Office for voluntary registration as per the settlement with General Smuts?
    (a) 3rd (b) 10th
    (c) 15th (d) 22nd

89. When Gandhiji regained consciousness after the murderous attack by a group of Pathans, led by Mir Alam, a friend took him to his home in a carriage and a doctor was called who stitched the wounds. Gandhiji stayed with him for about ten days. Who was this friend?
    (a) Parsee Rustomji (b) H.S.L. Polak
    (c) Joseph Doke (d) Essop Mian

90. On breach of faith on the part of General Smuts, Gandhiji appealed to his countrymen to burn publicly their registration certificates. On August 16, 1908 a public meeting was held at which over 2,000 certificates were burnt. This was the first bonfire in Gandhiji's political career. Identify the place of bonfire.
    (a) Johannesburg (b) Pretoria
    (c) Durban (d) None of these places

91. G.K. Gokhale came to South Africa from England on the invitation of Gandhiji in October

(a) 1909   (b) 1910
(c) 1911   (d) 1912

92. In the course of resistance against which of the following in South Africa did Gandhiji first use his new political weapon which came to be known later on as 'Satyagraha'?
   (a) Peace Preservation Ordinance
   (b) Natal Indenture Law
   (c) Asiatic Law Amendment Act
   (d) Immigrants Regulation Act

93. In connection with the South African struggle, another Indian deputation left for London in June, 1909 to represent the Indian case. The deputation consisted of two members, one was Gandhiji. Who was the other?
   (a) Sheth Haji Habib   (b) Abdul Gani
   (c) A.M. Cachalia   (d) Daud Mahomed

94. For the emancipation of Indian emigrants, Gandhiji organised two great protest marches in South Africa. One was in 1906. When was the other march organised?
   (a) 1909   (b) 1911
   (c) 1912   (d) 1913

95. Nearly what proportion of the actual resident Indian population of the Transvaal had been through the various prisons of the Transvaal during the *Satyagraha* struggle?
   (a) 50 per cent   (b) 33 per cent
   (c) 25 per cent   (d) 20 per cent

96. Kasturbai decided to join the Passive Resistance struggle in April, 1913. In which month of 1913 was she arrested?
    (a) July   (b) August
    (c) September   (d) October

97. With the declaration of strike by the indentured Indian workers at the coal mines of Newcastle, the *Satyagraha* struggle entered into its critical stage. When did the strike commence?
    (a) September 18, 1913   (b) October 10, 1913
    (c) October 17, 1913   (d) October 29, 1913

98. Touched by the appeal of women *satyagrahis* to go on strike, around how many indentured Indians at the coal-mines of Newcastle struck work?
    (a) 1,000   (b) 1,500
    (c) 2,000   (d) 3,000

99. About how many thousand Indians in the Transvaal were affected by the Asiatic Law Amendment Act which required registration of Indians with finger-prints like a criminal on pain of severe penalties?
    (a) Ten   (b) Eight
    (c) Six   (d) Four

100. Identify the year in which Gandhiji gave up both European dress and milk, and restricted himself to diet of fresh and dried fruits in South Africa.
    (a) 1912   (b) 1911
    (c) 1910   (d) 1909

101. Which of the following vows of self-suffering did Gandhiji impose upon himself to be observed in South Africa till the abolition of £ tax?

(a) To adopt labourer's dress
(b) To walk bare foot
(c) To have only one meal a day
(d) All the three

102. Gandhiji pleaded before the Government to pass special legislation to validate Indian marriages, but in vain. So *Satyagraha* by women was offered. They crossed over to the Transvaal in batches of
(a) Twenty   (b) Sixteen
(c) Twelve   (d) Ten

103. Searle's Supreme Court judgement which caused great resentment among Indians, leading to mass protests, related to
(a) Registration of Indians
(b) Strike by Indian coal miners
(c) Invalidation of Indian marriages
(d) None of the above

104. Who assumed the leadership of the 'army' of marching *satyagrahis* after Gandhiji's arrest?
(a) W.S.L. Polak   (b) P.K. Naidu
(c) H. Kallenbach   (d) Albert Christopher

105. Gandhiji's *Satyagraha* struggle in South Africa lasted for a period of about
(a) Six years   (b) Seven years
(c) Eight years   (d) Ten years

106. When was the *Satyagraha* struggle, launched by Gandhiji in South Africa, finally suspended following agreement with General Smuts, thus leading to the gradual release of *satyagrahis*?

(a) December 27, 1913   (b) January 21, 1914
(c) February 10, 1914   (d) February 25, 1914

107. The Indians' Relief Act was the first South African legislation designed to remove the grievances of the Indian settlers. It was passed in 1914 in the month of
(a) April   (b) May
(c) June   (d) July

108. Which of the following was not provided for in the Indian's Relief Act?
(a) Abolition of the system of indentured labour
(b) Legalising in South Africa all marriages legal in India
(c) Abolition of the £ 3 tax
(d) Making a domicile certificate bearing the holder's thumb impression sufficient evidence of right to enter the Union.

109. Having successfully finished the work that he had undertaken, Gandhiji left South Africa for good on
(a) June 10, 1914   (b) June 18, 1914
(c) July 4, 1914   (d) July 18, 1914

110. On the conclusion of struggle in South Africa, when Gandhiji sailed for England *en route* to India, he was accompanied by
(a) Kasturbai   (b) H. Kallenbach
(c) Both (a) and (b)   (d) Maganlal

3

Role in National Movement: Initial Phase

1. Gandhiji, the hero of the *Satyagraha* struggle of the Indians in South Africa, landed in Bombay on
   - (a) January 9, 1915
   - (b) January 26, 1915
   - (c) February 10, 1915
   - (d) February 20, 1915

2. Which of the following statements relating to the return of Gandhiji from South Africa is not correct?
   - (a) His landing took place at the Apollo Bunder — an honour shared by the Viceroys and India's most distinguished sons.
   - (b) He stayed at Santa Cruz in Jahangir Petit's house.
   - (c) As soon as he touched the Indian soil he took to *swadeshi* dress — a Kathaiwadi cloak, turban and *dhoti*.
   - (d) None of the above.

3. Who advised Gandhiji to remain as an observer and student in the country for a year before taking part in Indian politics?

41

(a) B.G. Tilak
(b) G.K. Gokhale
(c) Annie Besant
(d) Rabindranath Tagore

4. Soon after reaching Bombay from South Africa, Gandhiji went to Pune to meet the founder of the Servants of India Society for his advise. Who was he?

(a) A.V. Thakkar   (b) B.G. Tilak
(c) Pherozeshah Mehta   (d) G.K. Gokhale

5. Gandhiji's one year of political silence came to an end at the opening ceremony of the Benares Hindu University where he spoke on

(a) January 6, 1916   (b) January 26, 1916
(c) February 4, 1916   (d) March 15, 1916

6. Who drew the attention of Gandhiji to the hardships inflicted on the people at Viramgam of the notorious customs cordon and for the removal of which Gandhiji hinted to the possibility of launching of *satyagraha* in his speech?

(a) Mohanlal Panda   (b) Motilal
(c) Indulal Yajnik   (d) Mahadev Desai

7. One of the first problems that Gandhiji took up in the country to tackle was the abolition of the system of indentured labour. The system of exporting labourers from India on the indenture basis had come into existence as a result of the abolition of slavery in

(a) 1825   (b) 1833
(c) 1840   (d) 1852

8. Gandhiji began his campaign against indentured labour in the country by delivering the first of the series of public lectures in
   (a) Bombay   (b) Patna
   (c) Calcutta   (d) Gorakhpur

9. Favoured by Gandhiji, the Executive Committee of the Imperial Citizenship Association adopted the resolution in respect of the latest date during the year 1917 by which the abolition of the indenture system should be announced by the Government. Which was the latest date?
   (a) 15th June   (b) 1st July
   (c) 15th July   (d) 31st July

10. Public agitation and preparedness for *satyagraha* forced the Government to abolish the indenture system altogether on January 1,
    (a) 1918   (b) 1919
    (c) 1920   (d) 1921

11. Gandhiji's first major struggle in the country was staged on the soil of Champaran district in Bihar in 1917 in connection with indigo plantation. Who was largely instrumental in persuading Gandhiji to visit Champaran and lead the struggle over there?
    (a) Rajendra Prasad   (b) Raj Kumar Shukla
    (c) Dharnidhar   (d) Shambhu Saran

12. In which month of 1917 did Gandhiji leave for Champaran to study first hand the problem of indigo cultivators?
    (a) March   (b) April
    (c) May   (d) June

13. The cultivators engaged in the growing of indigo in the Champaran region suffered from many disabilities. One such disability was the forced indigo plantation on a certain proportion of their land. Identify that proportion.

(a) 1/4th
(b) 1/6th
(c) 1/3rd
(d) 3/20th

14. Accompanied by two local interpreters, Gandhiji left for the headquarters of the Champaran district to get first hand information about the hardships of the indigo growers. One was Dharnidhar. Who was the other?

(a) Ramnarain Prasad
(b) Braj Kishore Prasad
(c) Anugraha Narayan
(d) Raj Kumar Shukla

15. Who of the following was chosen by the associates of Gandhiji in the Champaran struggle to lead in case Gandhiji was jailed?

(a) Braj Kishore Prasad
(b) Mazharul Haque
(c) Both (a) and (b)
(d) Dharnidhar

16. Who acted as the contact man between Gandhiji and Sir Edwar Gait, the Lt-Governor of Bengal, resulting in the unconditional withdrawal of case against Gandhiji, thus enabling him to proceed with his work in Champaran?

(a) Madan Mohan Malaviya
(b) C.F. Andrews
(c) Anugraha Narain Sinha
(d) Rajendra Prasad

17. About how many peasants were examined and their statements recorded after careful cross-examination

by Gandhiji on the basis of which he prepared the famous survey of the Champaran struggle?

(a) 4,000   (b) 3,500

(c) 2,500   (d) 2,000

18. The Champaran Inquiry Committee was appointed by the Government of Bihar and Orissa on June 13, 1917 with Gandhiji as one of its members. The Committee was required to submit its report within

(a) One month   (b) Two months

(c) Three months   (d) Four months

19. The Government accepted all the recommendations of the Champaran Inquiry Committee. The Champaran Agrarian Bill, introduced on November 29, 1917 was passed and became an Act within a few months, thus marking an end of the struggle launched by Gandhiji. Who introduced the Bill?

(a) W. Manda   (b) W.H. Lewis

(c) E.H. Johnston   (d) J.A. Sweeny

20. Despite the solution of the problem of indigo cultivators, Gandhiji regarded his task at Champaran unfinished. In his opinion the main cause of the sufferings of the poor tenants was their ignorance. For its removal, he started a member of schools over there. The first school was started at

(a) Madhuban   (b) Barharwa

(c) Bhitharwa   (d) Belwa

21. While Gandhiji was still busy in his constructive work at Champaran, he had to rush to Ahmedabad in February 1918 to tackle the problem of textile workers in response to an appeal made by

(a) Shankarlal Banker   (b) Kaka Kalelkar
(c) Vallabhbhai Patel   (d) Anasuyabehn

22. Faced with labour problem, the textile millowners of Ahmedabad declared a lockout on February 22, 1918 which continued till
(a) March 2   (b) March 8
(c) March 11   (d) March 15

23. The dispute between the textile millowners of Ahmedabad and their workers was referred to arbitration. Who acted as the representative of the weavers?
(a) Gandhiji   (b) Shankarlal Banker
(c) Vallabhbhai Patel (d) All of the three

24. When the lockout of the textile mills of Ahmedabad was lifted by the mill-owners, the workers decided to go on strike, demanding an increase in their wages by
(a) 66 per cent   (b) 50 per cent
(c) 33 per cent   (d) 25 per cent

25. As the strike situation in Ahmedabad grew critical, Gandhiji resorted to fasting. His fast not only electrified the workers and restored their morale but also moved the millowners to agree to arbitration. Ultimately a settlement was reached in terms of which mill-owners agreed to increase the wages of workers by
(a) 25 per cent   (b) 30 per cent
(c) 35 per cent   (d) 40 per cent

26. Who in the end was appointed arbitrator to settle the labour dispute of textile industry at Ahmedabad?
    (a) Anand Shankar Dhruva
    (b) Chandulal Chamanlal
    (c) Amritlal Thakkar
    (d) None of the above

27. After how many days of strike was the settlement reached between Ahmedabad textile mill-owners and workers?
    (a) Twenty-five   (b) Twenty-one
    (c) Fifteen   (d) Twelve

28. Soon after the Ahmedabad weavers' strike ended, Gandhiji had to attend to the grievances of the peasants in the Kheda district of Gujarat. Who of the following had already inquired into the matter before Gandhiji arrived on the scene?
    (a) Amritlal Thakkar   (b) G.K. Deodhar
    (c) N.M. Joshi   (d) All of them

29. The cultivators of the Kheda district demanded the suspension of the land revenue assessment for the year because of the widespread failure of crops. They claimed that, as compared to the normal yield, the output during the year was less than
    (a) 25 per cent   (b) 33 per cent
    (c) 40 per cent   (d) 50 per cent

30. Gandhiji personally visited over fifty villages of the Kheda district and inspected closely the fields of the villagers. He came to the conclusion that the cultivators' demand was just. His final suggestion to the Government was to grant

(a) Full suspension
(b) Three-fourth suspension
(c) Half suspension
(d) One-third suspension

31. Who among the following principal comrades of
Gandhiji in the Kheda struggle had to suspend a
large and growing practice at the bar and which, for
all practical purposes, he was never able to resume?
(a) Indulal Yajnik   (b) Vallabhbhai Patel
(c) Shankarlal Banker   (d) G.K. Parekh

32. Through whom an agitation was set up in the
Bombay Legislative Council in connection with the
Kheda struggle?
(a) Vithalbhai Patel   (b) G.K. Parekh
(c) Both (a) and (b)   (d) Shankarlal Parekh

33. Despite several petitions and deputations, the
Government refused to grant the reasonable demand of the Kheda peasants. Thereupon Gandhiji
advised the cultivators to resort to *Satyagraha* from
a certain date in March, 1918. Identify the date
(a) 22nd   (b) 18th
(c) 12th   (d) 6th

34. The Government resorted to very coercive measures
for the realisation of land revenue from the
cultivators of the Kheda region. With a view to steel-
ing the hearts of frightened cultivators, Gandhiji
advised them to remove the crop of onion from a
field which, according to him, was wrongly
attached. A person volunteered to do this job. He
was convicted and sentenced to a brief term of

imprisonment. He earned from the people the honoured title of 'onion thief'. Who was he?

(a) Raj Kumar Shukla   (b) Deen Dayal
(c) Prem Kumar Mehta   (d) Mohanlal Pandya

35. The Kheda struggle lasted for about
    (a) Two months   (b) Four months
    (c) Five months   (d) Six months

36. Identify the place from where Gandhiji started his recruiting campaign for the War on behalf of the British Government.
    (a) Surat   (b) Ahmedabad
    (c) Kheda   (d) Rajkot

37. Gandhiji's participation in the war-effort as a recruiting sergeant on behalf of the British Government was an enigma to most of his friends and admirers. By recalling which of the following, he explained his point of view some years later?
    (a) "While as an individual I was opposed to war, I had no status for offering effective non-violent resistance."
    (b) "I had first to qualify for *swaraj* through the good offices of the statesmen of the empire and I could not qualify myself except through serving the empire in its life and death struggle."
    (c) "Non-violent resistance can only follow some real disinterested service, some heartfelt expression of love."
    (d) All of the above.

38. At which place did Gandhiji launch the first no-tax campaign in the country in 1918?

(a) Kheda   (b) Champaran
(c) Surat   (d) Bardoli

39. The Montagu-Chelmsford Report, which came out in July 1918, led to the expression of very conflicting opinions. Which of the following observations on the Report was made by Gandhiji?
    (a) "The scheme deserves sympathetic consideration, rather than summary rejection."
    (b) "A good report with a useless scheme."
    (c) "The political reforms included in the report were unworthy of England to give and India to take."
    (d) None of the above.

40. Gandhiji was startled by the recommendation of the Rowlatt Committee Report which he happened to read while he was convalescing in Ahmedabad. He first mentioned his apprehensions to
    (a) Shankarlal Banker   (b) Vallabhbhai Patel
    (c) Indulal Yajnik   (d) B.G. Horniman

41. To initiate and organise resistance against the passing of the notorious Rowlatt Bills, a small conference was held at Gandhiji's Sabarmati Ashram. Gandhiji drafted a *satyagraha* pledge. On which day of February 1919 was the *satyagraha* pledge signed?
    (a) 15th   (b) 20th
    (c) 24th   (d) 27th

42. How many persons signed the *satyagraha* pledge whom Gandhiji had called together in a small conference?
    (a) Twelve   (b) Sixteen
    (c) Twenty   (d) Twenty-four

43. In connection with the inauguration of the so-called *Rowlatt satyagraha*, Gandhiji started a Satyagraha Sabha in
    (a) Ahmedabad   (b) Bombay
    (c) Wardha   (d) Rajkot

44. The Rowlatt Bill No II was published as an Act on March 18, 1919. Late that night in the twilight condition of between sleep and consciousness, the idea of *hartal* broke upon Gandhiji. To whom in the early morning he first unfolded the plan of *hartal*?
    (a) C. Rajagopalachari
    (b) Mahadev Desai
    (c) Shankarlal Banker
    (d) Kasturi Ranga Iyanger

45. In observance of the call of *hartal* given by Gandhiji in March 1919, a huge procession was taken out in Chandni Chowk, Delhi. The police and military tried to disperse it, and even opened fire on it. A leader faced with bared chest the bayonets of the Gorkhas. Identify that leader.
    (a) Abdul Ghaffar Khan
    (b) Swami Shradhanand
    (c) Shaukat Ali
    (d) None of the above

46. Which of the following prohibited works of Gandhiji was selected by the Satyagraha Sabha for dissemination by the *satyagrahis* as a mark of civil disobedience in the context of Rowlatt agitation?
    (a) *Hind Swaraj*
    (b) *Sarvodaya*

(c) *The Story of a Satyagrahi*

(d) All of the three

47. As desired by the leaders of Punjab, Gandhiji started for Delhi and Amritsar on April 8, 1919. On the way he was served with a written order, prohibiting his entry into Delhi and Punjab. On his refusal to get down from the train, he was taken out of the train at one of the railway stations, put under police custody and forcibly taken to Bombay where he was set free. Identify the railway station.

(a) Mathura
(b) Palwal
(c) Agra
(d) Sawai Madhopur

48. On April 14, 1919 Gandhiji addressed a huge meeting and upbraided the people for their violence. He declared a three days' penitential fast for himself as also appealed to the audience to observe a similar fast for one day. Where did this meeting take place?

(a) Ahmedabad
(b) Bombay
(c) Delhi
(d) Amritsar

49. Identify the place where Gandhiji first coined the expression "Himalayan miscalculation" which gained wide currency afterward

(a) Bombay
(b) Ahmedabad
(c) Nadiad
(d) Wardha

50. In respect of which of the following did Gandhiji confess his grave error publicly and regarded it as an "Himalayan miscalculation" on his part?

(a) In calling upon the people in the Kheda district and elsewhere to launch upon civil disobedience.

(b) His lending support to the war-effort of the British Government.

(c) His admission of an untouchable family to the Sabarmati Ashram.

(d) None of the above.

51. Gandhiji regarded his participation in 1919 session of the Congress as his real entrance into the Congress politics. Where was this session of the Congress held?
   (a) Lahore   (b) Amritsar
   (c) Calcutta   (d) Lucknow

52. Gandhiji attended the Indian National Congress for the first time in
   (a) 1915   (b) 1910
   (c) 1906   (d) 1901

53. To defy the Government orders, Gandhiji published an unregistered weekly *Satyagraha* in
   (a) 1919   (b) 1920
   (c) 1921   (d) 1922

54. For quite some time following the Jallianwala Bagh massacre Gandhiji, despite repeated requests, was not allowed to enter the Punjab. His request to visit the Punjab was at last granted by the Viceroy. In which month of 1919 he was able to go there and joined the leaders who were already there?
   (a) July   (b) August
   (c) September   (d) October

55. Which of the following suggestions was not put forward by Gandhiji and other Congress leaders to

cooperate with the Hunter Inquiry Committee by the Viceroy to investigate the Punjab disturbances?

(a) Leaders should be released pending inquiry.

(b) Both the revision judges should be from outside the Punjab.

(c) Congress Committee should be permitted to lead evidence and cross-examine the witnesses of the other side.

(d) Revision judges should have power to receive and call further evidence where they think necessary.

56. The Indian National Congress set up a separate Committee of Inquiry to look into the Punjab attrocities. The main responsibility of organising the work of the Congress Committee devolved on Gandhiji. The Committee took evidence of 1700 persons. Its unanimous report was submitted in 1920 in the month of

(a) January   (b) February

(c) March   (d) April

57. According to Gandhiji, the *Khilafat* issue offered a golden opportunity for the promotion of Hindu-Muslim unity in the country. He urged Hindus to lend full support to the Indian Muslims on this issue. The *Khilafat* issue related to the policy of the British Government towards

(a) Turkey   (b) Afghanistan

(c) Iraq   (d) Iran

58. Gandhiji was elected President of the All-India *Khilafat* Conference which held its session on 24 November, 1919 at

(a) Lahore   (b) Delhi
(c) Bombay   (d) Amritsar

59. Which of the following statements about *Khilafat* Movement and Gandhiji is not correct?
   (a) Gandhiji used the platform of the *Khilafat* Movement to declare non-cooperation against the Government.
   (b) Gandhiji issued a Manifesto on March 10, 1920, embodying his ideas on the future course of action to be pursued by the *Khilafatists* if their demands were not granted.
   (c) Gandhiji placed the *Khilafat* problem on the same level of political importance as the Home Rule for India.
   (d) None of the above.

60. Prior to Gandhiji's active participation in the Congress affairs, there was no full-fledged constitution of the Congress. There existed just a few rules for running the Congress machinery which had been framed by
   (a) Dadabhai Naoroji
   (b) G.K. Gokhale
   (c) Surendranath Banerjee
   (d) B.G. Tilak

61. Gandhiji was given the responsibility of framing the constitution of the Congress. Two persons were associated with him in this constitution-making work. One was N.C. Kelkar. Who was the other?
   (a) I.B. Sen
   (b) C.R. Das

(c) Motilal Nehru

(d) Madan Mohan Malaviya

62. In the constitution presented by Gandhiji, the goal of the Congress was the attainment of *swaraj* within the British Empire, if possible and without it if necessary. At which session of the Congress was the draft of the constitution, prepared by Gandhiji, finally adopted?

(a) Calcutta   (b) Allahabad

(c) Nagpur   (d) Amritsar

63. In April 1921 Gandhiji launched the programme of

(a) Enlisting a crore of members in the Congress.

(b) Raising Rs one crore for Tilak Swaraj Fund.

(c) Setting up 20 lakh *charkhas* in the country in the furtherance of national constructive programme.

(d) All of the above.

64. On which day in August 1920 Gandhiji gave the signal for the non-cooperation campaign by his letter written to the Viceroy, surrendering his decorations and titles?

(a) 1st   (b) 8th

(c) 15th   (d) 22nd

65. The special session of the Indian National Congress in September 1920 accepted Gandhiji's programme of non-cooperation to secure redress of Punjab and *Khilafat* wrongs. Where was this special session held?

(a) Delhi   (b) Bombay

(c) Calcutta   (d) Ahmedabad

66. Who of the following leaders, in particular, wanted the demand for *swaraj* to be included in Gandhiji's non-cooperation resolution, which Gandhiji readily agreed and the resolution was passed unanimously by the Congress in 1920 at its annual session held in Nagpur?
    (a) Motilal Nehru
    (b) C. Vijayaraghvachari
    (c) C.R. Das
    (d) Both (a) and (b)

67. Gandhiji's proposal regarding boycott of the Legislative Councils was strongly challenged by a leader thus: "These (reforms) are not the gifts of the British Government. Reforms have been wrung out of the hands of the British Government. I want to make the Councils an instrument for the attainment of *swaraj* and to use the weapon which is in hollow of your hands to bring about the full, complete *swaraj*." Identify him
    (a) C.R. Das
    (b) Lajpat Rai
    (c) Motilal Nehru
    (d) B.C. Pal

68. When did Gandhiji make this observation that if the people scrupulously followed his programme, *swaraj* should dawn within a year?
    (a) 1918
    (b) 1920
    (c) 1922
    (d) 1924

69. From which place in Gujarat did Gandhiji decide to launch the civil disobedience movement?
    (a) Rajkot
    (b) Bardoli
    (c) Kheda
    (d) Surat

70. Before the civil disobedience or non-cooperation movement could be effectively launched, Gandhiji

suspended it because of an outbreak of mob violence at Chauri Chaura in the sate of
(a) Gujarat   (b) Uttar Pradesh
(c) Punjab   (d) Bihar

71. How many members of the police force were burnt alive by the mob in the Chauri Chaura incident which led Gandhiji to suspend the civil disobedience movement?
(a) Eleven   (b) Eighteen
(c) Twenty   (d) Twenty-seven

72. The Congress Working Committee endorsed Gandhiji's decision to suspend the civil disobedience and in its place opted for a constructive programme at its meeting held on February 12, 1922 at
(a) Delhi   (b) Bardoli
(c) Ahmedabad   (d) Bombay

73. The suspension of civil disobedience by Gandhiji came as a shock to large many national leaders. One of them from prison in an indignant letter asked him: "Why should a town at the foot of the Himalayas be penalised if a village at Cape Comorin failed to non-violence? Isolate Chauri Chaura and Gorakhpur, but go on with civil disobedience, individual and mass." Identify him.
(a) Motilal Nehru   (b) Lajpat Rai
(c) Vallabhbhai Patel   (d) M.A. Ansari

74. Who called the dropping of civil disobedience by Gandhiji as a "national calamity""
(a) Jawaharlal Nehru   (b) M.N. Roy
(c) Subhas Chandra Bose (d) C.R. Das

75. At which place was Gandhiji arrested for the first time by the British Government for sedition?
    (a) Bombay   (b) Delhi
    (c) Wardha   (d) Ahmedabad

76. Who of the following leaders of the bar, enjoying princely income, heralded the boycott of legal profession on the call given by Gandhiji?
    (a) Motilal Nehru   (b) C.R. Das
    (c) Both (a) and (b)   (d) Tej Bahadur Sapru

77. For writing which of the following articles, published in *Young India,* was Gandhiji convicted for the first time in the country by the Government?
    (a) *Tampering with Loyalty*
    (b) *The Puzzle and its Solution*
    (c) *Shaking the Manes*
    (d) All the three

78. Identify the four-year period during which Gandhiji had resolved not to enter into any political questions or do anything to oppose the Government, but to use his time for 'constructive programme'.
    (a) 1922-26   (b) 1923-27
    (c) 1924-28   (d) 1925-29

79. How many items were listed down by Gandhiji for the 'constructive programme'?
    (a) Seven   (b) Nine
    (c) Eleven   (d) Thirteen

80. At which session of the All India Congress Committee, held towards the end of June 1924, did Gandhiji declare himself as "defeated and humbled"?

(a) Delhi   (b) Ahmedabad
(c) Bombay   (d) Nagpur

81. A wave of violent communal riots swept over the country in 1924 on account of which Gandhiji felt very much upset and was in great distress, knowing not what to do. The terrible riots that broke out at a particular place led Gandhiji to do penance by observing a fast for 21 days. Which was that place?
(a) Kohat   (b) Sambhal
(c) Gulbarga   (d) Aligarh

82. The twenty-one day fast of September 1924 by Gandhiji to bring about Hindu-Muslim unity, which he considered essential for the country's freedom, was undertaken in Delhi at the residence of
(a) G.D. Birla
(b) Mahomed Ali
(c) Shaukat Ali
(d) Swami Shradhanand

83. At whose insistence did Gandhiji agree to preside over the Belgaum session of the Congress held in December 1924 which ratified the Gandhi-Nehru-Das Pact and altered the Congress franchise, making spinning a qualification instead of four annas per year?
(a) Jawaharlal Nehru
(b) Abul Kalam Azad
(c) C.R. Das
(d) C.Y. Chintamani

84. Identify the incorrect statement.
(a) Gandhiji hailed the Kanpur session of the Congress, held in the last week of December 1925,

as a landmark in Indian history because an Indian woman was elected to preside for the first time.

(b) Gandhiji was released on February 5, 1924 for reasons of health.

(c) Gandhiji characterised Katherine Mayo's book, *Mother India*, as a "Drain Inspector's Report."

(d) None of the above

85. At which session of the Congress, held in December 1928, Gandhiji moved his resolution in favour of Independence if Dominion Status was not granted by the end of 1929?
    (a) Calcutta   (b) Madras
    (c) Ahmedabad   (d) Lucknow

86. At Gandhiji's instance the Lahore Congress session of 1929 held that *Swaraj* in Congress creed shall mean *Purna Swaraj* or Complete Independence. Who presided over this session?
    (a) Subhas Chandra Bose (b) Jawaharlal Nehru
    (c) Abul Kalam Azad   (d) M.A. Ansari

87. The Congress Working Committee at its meeting held on February 15, 1929 accepted the foreign cloth boycott scheme and appointed the Foreign Cloth Boycott Committee with Gandhiji as Chairman. Where was this meeting held?
    (a) Delhi   (b) Ahmedabad
    (c) Madras   (d) Patna

88. Gandhiji regarded the boycott of foreign cloth not merely boycott but considered it indispensable for the attainment of *Swaraj* in terms of the hungry millions. He appealed to the people to give up the use

of foreign cloth and organised on March 4, 1929 a foreign cloth burning demonstration at the Shraddhanand Park,

(a) Allahabad   (b) Amritsar

(c) Calcutta   (d) Bombay

89. Gandhiji was appointed as Congress Dictator to launch Civil Disobedience Movement by the All India Congress Committee in

(a) November, 1929   (b) December, 1929

(c) January, 1930   (d) February, 1930

90. Gandhiji was prepared to put off civil disobedience if the British Government were to grant the substance of self-government. How many needs or demands were listed down by Gandhiji for immediate fulfilment on the part of the Government which, in his view, would mean the substance of independence?

(a) Thirteen   (b) Eleven

(c) Nine   (d) Seven

91. On which day of March 1930 Gandhiji started with a band of chosen volunteers on his famous Dandi March to break the law by manufacturing illegally, but openly, salt from the sea?

(a) Sixth   (b) Eighth

(c) Tenth   (d) Twelfth

92. How many *satyagrahis* accompanied Gandhiji when he started on his historic march, through the Gujarat villages, to Dandi on the sea coast?

(a) 78   (b) 71

(c) 66   (d) 51

93. In how many days was the 241 mile-journey from Sabarmati Ashram to Dandi covered on foot by Gandhiji and his volunteers?
    - (a) 20
    - (b) 24
    - (c) 28
    - (d) 30

94. How old was Gandhiji when he started on the historic Dandi March?
    - (a) 65 years
    - (b) 63 years
    - (c) 61 years
    - (d) 59 years

95. Who was nominated by Gandhiji to lead the *satyagrahis* on the Dandi March in the event of his arrest?
    - (a) Jawaharlal Nehru
    - (b) Vithalbhai Patel
    - (c) Abdul Ghaffar Khan
    - (d) Abbas Tyabji

95. Jawaharlal Nehru was arrested on April 14, 1930 during the agitation for the abolition of Salt Tax and was sentenced to six months' imprisonment under the Salt Act. When was Gandhiji arrested in this connection?
    - (a) April 10, 1930
    - (b) April 20, 1930
    - (c) April 28, 1930
    - (d) May 4, 1930

96. Gandhiji's arrest during Salt *satyagraha* led to *hartals* and strikes all over the country. The revolutionary zeal was at its zenith. At one place the people took possession of the town, replaced the police and established their own rule for a week until the martial was imposed. Which was that town?
    - (a) Surat
    - (b) Sholapur
    - (c) Rajkot
    - (d) Porbandar

97. Who described Gandhi's march to Dandi in the following words?

"Like the historic march of Ramchandra to Lanka, the march of Gandhi will be memorable."

(a) Motilal Nehru
(b) Sarojini Naidu
(c) Vallabhbhai Patel
(d) Madan Mohan Malaviya

98. Which of the following statements in respect of Gandhi's Dandi March is not correct?

(a) The first batch of *satyagrahis* included Mira-behn and Reginald Reynolds.
(b) The ages of *satyagrahis* varied from sixteen to sixty-one
(c) Monday was observed as a day of rest during the Dandi March.
(d) Gandhiji was arrested before he could offer *satyagraha* and make salt at the government depot at Bharsana.

4

Role in National Movement:
Later Phase

1. On which day of February 1931 did the negotiation
   for settlement between Gandhiji and Lord Irwin, the
   Viceroy, commence?
   (a) 10th   (b) 15th
   (c) 17th   (d) 21st

2. How many demands were put forward by Gandhiji
   before Lord Irwin, as the absolute minimum, for
   peace negotiations to begin?
   (a) Four   (b) Six
   (c) Eight   (d) Ten

3. During the period of negotiations with the Viceroy,
   Gandhiji and most of the Congress Working Committee members stayed at the house of
   (a) G.D. Birla   (b) Jamnadas Mehta
   (c) Asaf Ali   (d) M.A. Ansari

4. When was the Gandhi-Irwin Pact signed?
   (a) March 2, 1931   (b) March 5, 1931
   (c) March 15, 1931   (d) March 25, 1931

5. Despite widespread resentment and unhappiness, the Congress endorsed the Gandhi-Irwin Pact on March 29, 1931 at its annual session held at
   (a) Karachi   (b) Lahore
   (c) Bombay   (d) Calcutta

6. Identify the concession granted by the Government under the Gandhi-Irwin Pact.
   (a) Permission for peaceful picketing without any violation of ordinary laws
   (b) Permission to collect or make salt for one's use
   (c) Both (a) and (b)
   (d) Payment of reparations to those whose lands had been confiscated

7. Which of the following was not a part of the Gandhi-Irwin Pact?
   (a) Discontinuance of the Civil Disobedience Movement.
   (b) Federation as an essential part of the scheme of constitutional reforms.
   (c) Steps to be taken for the participation of the Congress in the future discussions on the scheme of constitutional reform.
   (d) Amnesty to political prisoners who had been convicted for violence under the Special Ordinances.

8. Who was the President of the Congress at the time Gandhi-Irwin agreement was reached?
   (a) Abul Kalam Azad
   (b) Jawaharlal Nehru
   (c) Rajendra Prasad
   (d) Madan Mohan Malaviya

9. Who made the following observation on the Gandhi-Irwin Pact?

"Was it for this that our people had so gallantly fought for a year? Were all our brave words and deeds to end in this? The independence resolution of the Congress, the pledge of January 26, so often repeated? So I lay and pondered on that March night, and in my heart there was a great emptiness as of something precious gone, almost beyond recall."

(a) Jawaharlal Nehru   (b) C.R. Das
(c) Subhas Chandra Bose (d) Vallabhbhai Patel

10. Lord Willingdon succeeded Lord Irwin as the new Viceroy in April 1931. Meanwhile reports were reaching Gandhiji about serious violations of the Agreement he had made with Lord Irwin. Gandhiji wired to the Viceroy for an interview in this connection and met him at Simla along with

(a) Prabhushankar Patkani
(b) Jawaharlal Nehru
(c) Vallabhbhai Patel
(d) All of them

11. Following the talk between Lord Willingdon and Gandhiji, a communique was published on August 28, 1931 which is often called as "second settlement". Which of the following was not provided for in this settlement?

(a) Congress would be represented at the Round Table Conference by Gandhiji.
(b) Earlier settlement of 5th March would be operative.

(c) No enquiry would be held in respect of the repression in Bardoli.

(d) Future complaints would be dealt with ordinary administrative procedure.

12. Identify the Muslim nationalist leader who, according to the original plan, was to accompany Gandhiji as a delegate to the Second Round Table Conference, but the Viceroy did not nominate him.
   (a) M.A. Ansari   (b) Abul Kalam Azad
   (c) Asaf Ali   (d) Abdul Ghaffar Khan

13. Who among the following was not in the party that accompanied Gandhiji to participate in the Second Round Table Conference?
   (a) Sarojini Naidu   (h) Mirabehn
   (c) Vallabhbhai Patel   (d) Mahadev Desai

14. Who acted as Gandhiji's adviser at the Second Round Table Conference?
   (a) G.D. Birla
   (b) Madan Mohan Malaviya
   (c) Prabhashankar Patkani
   (d) Sarojini Naidu

15. While in London for taking part in the Second Round Table Conference, Gandhiji stayed at the Kingsley Hall Settlement in the East End as the guest of
   (a) Muriel Lester   (b) Gilbert Murray
   (c) Lloyd George   (d) Harold Laski

16. To identify himself with the poor millions of India, Gandhiji, while in London in connection with the Second Round Table Conference, not only spun

everyday, but gave strict instructions to Mirabehn to ensure that the daily expenditure on his food should never exceed

(a) 2s.6d   (b) 2s.2d

(c) 1s.6d   (d) 1s.2d

17. Though at the Round Table Conference in London Gandhiji could gain nothing, he was the richer for having secured many friends and the goodwill of the people. Who of the following eminent persons refused to meet him?

(a) Winston Churchill   (b) Lloyd George

(c) Gilbert Murray   (d) Lady Astor

18. Identify the incorrect statement in respect of Gandhiji and the Round Table Conference that he attended.

(a) In his first spech at the Conference Gandhiji said that the Congress stood for central responsibility, Indian fedderation and safe-guards in 'her interest'.

(b) B.R. Ambedkar put forward before the Minorities Committee the demand for separate electorates for the depressed classes which was supported by all other minorities.

(c) M.A. Jinnah and B.R. Ambedkar denied Gandhiji's claim to speak for the whole of India.

(d) None of the above.

19. The Second Round Table Conference, which Gandhiji attended as the sole delegate of the Congress, did not, on the whole, make any marked progress in respect of its main work. Identify its main work.

(a) Completion of the structure of federal judiciary and federal legislature.

(b) Distribution of financial resources between the Centre and Provinces.

(c) Mode of accession of States to Federation.

(d) All of the above.

20. While Gandhiji was in London to take part in deliberations at the Round Table Conference, the Willingdon Government in India had gone back upon its word and had launched a campaign of repression. In which of the following areas had inhuman brutalities been perpetrated by the police?

(a) N.W.F.P.   (b) U.P.
(c) Bengal   (d) All the three

21. Who among the following national leaders was arrested by the Government even before Gandhiji's arrival in the country from London?

(a) Jawaharlal Nehru
(b) Purushottam Das Tandon
(c) Both (a) and (b)
(d) Vallabhbhai Patel

22. Before re-starting *Satyagraha*, Gandhiji drew the attention of the Viceroy to the policy of repression and the acquiring by the Government of extraordinary powers through the issue of special ordinances. But the Viceroy refused to listen and grant an interview. Instead Gandhiji was arrested on the morning of January 4, 1932 at

(a) Bombay   (b) Ahmedabad
(c) Delhi   (d) Wardha

23. The President of the Indian National Congress was also arrested along with Gandhiji on January 4, 1932. Who was he?
    (a) Jawaharlal Nehru   (b) Vallabhbhai Patel
    (c) Rajendra Prasad   (d) M.A. Ansari

24. Some of the leaders, particularly the General Secretary of the Congress, held the view that since the country was exhausted after the 1930 repression, the response to *Satyagraha* would be poor. Identify the person who was the General Secretary.
    (a) Syed Mahmud
    (b) J.B. Kripalani
    (c) Maulana Abul Kalam Azad
    (d) Mahadev Desai

25. From Yeravda jail where he was taken as a state prisoner after his arrest on January 4, 1932, Gandhiji wrote to the Government on March 11, 1932 about the brutal repression that had crossed all legitimate bounds and also gave a warning that in the event of creating separate electorate for the depressed classes he would fast unto death. This letter was addressed to
    (a) Viceroy
    (b) British Prime Minister
    (c) Secretary of state
    (d) Home Member

26. Despite Gandhiji's protest and threat to fast unto death, Ramsay MacDonald announced the Communal Award on
    (a) June 7, 1932   (b) July 10, 1932
    (c) July 30, 1932   (d) August 17, 1932

27. Identify the leader of the untouchables who repudiated B.R. Ambedkar and condemned the Communal Award, popularly known as MacDonald Award.
    (a) Jagjivan Ram   (b) M.C. Rajah
    (c) B.S. Kamath   (d) None of the above

28. As a protest of Ramsay MacDonald's Communal Award, which threatened to separate the so-called untouchables from the Hindu society, Gandhiji's historic fast unto death at the Yeravda jail commenced on
    (a) September 4, 1932   (b) September 10, 1932
    (c) September 15, 1932   (d) September 20, 1932

29. The provision of separate electorates for the Depressed Classes forced Gandhiji to undertake fast unto death. As an alternative, a system of primary and secondary election for a limited number of seats was put forward which, while maintaning the principle of joint electorates, would enable the Depressed classes to choose their own candidates. Gandhiji was prepared to consider this plan favourably. Who made this proposal?
    (a) Tej Bahadur Sapru   (b) Chimanlal Setalvad
    (c) Rajendra Prasad   (d) C. Rajagopalachari

30. The Poona or Yeravda Pact was the immediate outcome of the fast that Gandhiji had undertaken on the issue of the Communal Award and it was only after it had been signed by all the parties concerned that paved the way for him to break his fast. The draft of the Pact was prepared by
    (a) M.R. Jayakar   (b) A.V. Thakkar
    (c) H. Kunzru   (d) M.C. Rajah

31. Ramsay MacDonald's Communal Award allotted 71 seats for the Depressed Classes in the provincial legislatures. How many seats were awarded to the Depressed Classes under the Poona Pact which was evolved in place of the Communal Award?

    (a) 71   (b) 125
    (c) 147   (d) 197

32. Identify the leader who was critical of Gandhiji's fast unto death on the Communal Award because he considered it a religious and sentimental approach to a political question, but who in the end conceded: "What a magician! I thought he was a little man sitting in Yeravda prison. And how well he knew how to pull the strings that move people's hearts!"

    (a) Jawaharlal Nehru
    (b) Subhas Chandra Bose
    (c) Maulana Abul Kalam Azad
    (d) None of the above

33. Who made the following appeal to the countrymen while addressing a public meeting in Poona when Gandhiji broke his fast unto death that he had undertaken in the Yeravda prison for the cause of untouchables?

    "Today in our determined effort, let us all join Mahatmaji in his noble task of removing the burden of ages, the burden of disrespect upon the bent back of those who have been stigmatized for the accident of their birth, and the sinful denial, to a large body of our countrymen, of sympathy which is the birth right of all human beings. We are not only casting off the chain of India's moral enslavement, but indicating the path for all humanity."

(a) Shaukat Ali
(b) Rabindranath Tagore
(c) A.V. Thakkar
(d) Madan Mohan Malviya

34. In February 1933 Gandhiji started the publication of a weekly paper, *Harijan*, to promote the anti-untouchability campaign. Its first issue was out on February 11, 1933 from
(a) Wardha   (b) Ahmedabad
(c) Poona   (d) Delhi

35. After about how many years of its existence was the Sabarmati Ashram disbanded by Gandhiji?
(a) Fourteen   (b) Sixteen
(c) Eighteen   (d) Twenty

36. On which day of May 1933 was Gandhi's second civil disobedience movement suspended for six weeks with an appeal to the people to use this period in the service of the Harijans?
(a) 7th   (b) 9th
(c) 13th   (d) 15th

37. Who was the President of the Indian National Congress when the civil disobedience movement was suspended in May 1933?
(a) M.S. Aney   (b) M.A. Ansari
(c) Jawaharlal Nehru   (d) Vallabhbhai Patel

38. Gandhi's decision to suspend the civil disobedience movement in May 1933 upset many Congress leaders. Two of them denounced it in these words: "The latest act of Mahatma Gandhi in suspending civil disobedience is a confession of failure. We are of the

opinion that the Mahatma, as a political leader, has failed. The time has now come for a radical reorganisation of the Congress on new principles with a new method for which a new leader is essential, as it is unfair to expect the Mahatma to work a programme not consistent with his lifelong principles." One of them was Subhas Chandra Bose. Who was the other?

(a) C. Rajagopalachari   (b) C.R. Das
(c) Vallabhbhai Patel   (d) Vithalbhai Patel

39. Gandhiji's last civil disobedience campaign, which was resumed after the failure of the Second Round Table Conference in London when he returned to India towards the end of 1931, continued till

(a) May, 1934   (b) February, 1934
(c) November, 1933   (d) October, 1933

40. On July 30, 1933 Gandhiji informed the Government of Bombay of his decision to march from Ahmedabad to Ras to revive civil disobedience movement. How many followers were chosen to accompany him?

(a) Thirty-three   (b) Twenty-five
(c) Twenty-one   (d) Eighteen

41. Gandhiji accorded very high priority to the removal of untouchability in his plan of action for the country's march towards freedom and progress. To create awareness in this regard, he went on an all-India tour in 1933 in the month of

(a) May   (b) July
(c) September   (d) November

42. Gandhiji's famous Harijan-uplift tour started from
    (a) Ahmedabad   (b) Wardha
    (c) Bombay   (d) Delhi

43. Identify the place in Orissa where Gandhiji re-
    nounced the use of conveyance for the rest of the
    Harijan tour in Orissa and decided to go on foot to
    address public meetings.
    (a) Cuttack   (b) Chandanpur
    (c) Puri   (d) Bhubhneshwar

44. At which place on June 25, 1934 was a bomb
    thrown on Gandhiji's car during the Harijan tour,
    Gandhiji escaping narrowly?
    (a) Nagpur   (b) Pune
    (c) Ranchi   (d) Varanasi

45. On his Harijan tour Gandhiji covered more than
    12,500 miles and collected about Rs 8 lakhs for the
    Harijan cause. The tour lasted for about
    (a) Five months   (b) Seven months
    (c) Nine months   (d) One year

46. Identify the place where Gandhiji's Harijan tour ter-
    minated.
    (a) Allahabad   (b) Varanasi
    (c) Wardha   (d) Delhi

47. A poor man at Kalol threw a cowrie in the collec-
    tions for the Harijan fund. Gandhiji regarded it as
    more precious than gold. He offered the cowrie for
    auction at a public meeting which fetched Rs. 111.
    Identify the place of this public meeting.
    (a) Nagpur   (b) Ahmedabad
    (c) Amraoti   (d) Bhopal

48. Gandhiji began the Harijan uplift work in the country when he brought the resolution to remove untouchability before the Congress in
    (a) 1926   (b) 1924
    (c) 1922   (d) 1920

49. Pandit Lalnath, leader of the Santanists, received a lathi blow on his head when he tried to address a meeting, organised for Gandhiji, condemning the Harijan movement. On his arrival at the meeting place, Gandhiji not only rebuked the audience and called upon Pandit Lalnath to speak, but also imposed upon himself a fast of seven seven days as a penance. Identify the place of incident.
    (a) Poona   (b) Bhavnagar
    (c) Ajmer   (d) Ahmedabad

50. Which day of July 1934 was observed throughout the country as a day of thanksgiving for the successful termination of the Harijan tour undertaken by Gandhiji?
    (a) 12th   (b) 18th
    (c) 22nd   (d) 29th

51. While Gandhiji was in the midst of his hectic tour of South India in connection with the Harijan uplift work, he received the news of terrible earthquake which shook North Bihar on January 15, 1934. When did Gandhiji reached Patna, the centre of relief work in Bihar?
    (a) January 26, 1934   (b) February 10, 1934
    (c) February 24, 1934   (d) March 11, 1934

52. To whom did Gandhiji write these words when he was informed telegraphically about the havoc caused by the earthquake in Bihar?

"What shall I write? What comfort I shall give? I have been upset, and to give up what I am doing looks like *adharma*."

(a) Jagjivan Ram
(b) Rajendra Prasad
(c) Deepnarayan Singh
(d) J.B. Kripalani

53. In a statement relating to Bihar earthquake, Gandhiji had said that the calamity that had befallen Bihar was a "retribution of the sin of untouchability". This brought a sharp rejoinder from an eminent personality who observed: "It has caused me a painful surprise to find Mahatma Gandhi accusing those who blindly follow their own social custom of untouchability, of having brought down God's vengeance upon certain parts of Bihar, evidently, specially selected, for His desolating displeasure." Identify the person.

(a) Rabindranath Tagore
(b) Jawaharlal Nehru
(c) Madan Mohan Malaviya
(d) C. Rajagopalachari

54. In his long statement of September 17, 1934 Gandhiji confirmed his intention to retire from the Congress, giving reasons for the same. From where was this statement issued?

(a) Ahmedabad
(b) Wardha
(c) Poona
(d) New Delhi

55. Identify the leader to whom Gandhiji wrote these lines in September 1934 about his retirement from the Congress.

"I fear none of the consequences dreaded by some friends, for I know my ground. A tree is no more hurt by a ripe fruit falling from it than would the Congress by my going out of it. Indeed the fruit would be dead weight, if it did not fall when it was fully ripe. Mine is that condition. I feel that I am a dead weight on the Congress now."

(a) Jawaharlal Nehru   (b) Sarojini Naidu

(c) Vallabhbhai Patel   (d) G.B. Pant

56. The Congress at its annual session held in Bombay in October 1934, adopted the following resolution in regard to Gandhiji's decision to retire from the Congress: "This Congress reiterates its confidence in the leadership of Mahatma Gandhi and .... while reluctantly accepting his decision, places on record its deep sense of gratitude for the unique services rendered by him to the nation and notes with satisfaction his assurance that his advice and guidance will be available to the Congress whenever necessary." Who was the Congress President at this historic session?

(a) Rajendra Prasad   (b) M.A. Ansari

(c) Abul Kalam Azad   (d) Vallabhbhai Patel

57. Who among the following leaders suggested to Gandhiji an intermediate course of remaining in the Congress without participating in any active administration of the organisation?

(a) G.B. Pant   (b) Rafi Ahmad Kidwai

(c) Abul Kalam Azad   (d) Both (a) and (b)

58. On his release from prison in 1934 Jawaharlal Nehru wrote to Gandhiji a bitter but powerfully argued letter. Which of the following was attacked by him in his letter?
    (a) The manner in which civil disobedience was abandoned.
    (b) Adoption of the parliamentary programme.
    (c) Congress slowly turning itself into a 'caucus' from top to bottom.
    (d) All of the above.

59. Welcoming the rise of the Socialist Party in the Congress, Gandhiji sent to its chairman in August 1934 a cursory criticism of the programme so as to help organise its effort. Who was then the chairman of the Congress Socialist Party?
    (a) M.R. Masani
    (b) Acharya Narendra Dev
    (c) Jayprakash Narayan
    (d) Ram Manohar Lohia

60. With the suspension of the civil disobedience movement by Gandhiji, the demand for Council entry was again put forward. Gandhiji himself also felt that it would be good for some politicians to engage themselves with work in the Councils. Who of the following came to Patna on August 4, 1934 to discuss with Gandhiji the proposal for the revival of the Swaraj Party and for the participation in the next general elections?
    (a) Bhulabhai Desai   (b) M.A. Ansari
    (c) B.C. Roy   (d) All of the three

61. In April 1936 Gandhiji decided to live in a village to appreciate the problems of villagers better as also to use it as a laboratory for his experiments. Gandhiji selected the village, Segaon, for his residence and renamed it Sevagram. Who of the following was already living and working there?
    (a) Mirabehn   (b) J.C. Kumarappa
    (c) Jamnalal Bajaj   (d) None of the above

62. Having divested himself of the responsibility of leadership of the Congress, Gandhiji gave full attention to the revitalisation of rural India and the organisation of the All-India Village Industries Association. Which of the following became the headquarters of training and research in village industries?
    (a) Sevagram   (b) Maganwadi
    (c) Sabarmati   (d) Faizpur

63. It was from Sevagram that Gandhiji enunciated and announced his new educational system and later founded the Talimi Sangh. Interesting experiments in education were carried out at Sevagram under the direction and guidance of
    (a) Aryanayakan   (b) Asha Devi
    (c) Both (a) and (b)   (d) Jamnalal Bajaj

64. Gandhiji presided over the Educational Conference held on October 22, 1937 where he outlined his much debated scheme of education through basic crafts. Identify the place of the Conference.
    (a) Wardha   (b) Ahmedabad
    (c) Bardoli   (d) Belgaum

65. Gandhiji's main interest in the formation of Congress ministries in 1937 in a number of provinces

was the implementation of the programme for the reconstruction of the country. He advised the ministers to lead a life of simplicity and wanted them to take a maximum salary of Rupees

(a) Two hundred   (b) Three hundred
(c) Four hundred   (d) Five hundred

66. The Thakore Saheb of Rajkot, as the ruler of the state was called, had agreed to appoint a commission with a majority of nationalists on it, to go into the question of constitutional reforms. Later he backed out. Thereupon Gandhiji went on a fast. For how many days did his fast last?

(a) Fifteen   (b) Ten
(c) Seven   (d) Four

67. Which of the following statements in respect of Gandhiji and the Rajkot agitation for constitutional reforms is not correct?

(a) Gandhiji sent Kasturbai to court arrest in Rajkot in early February, 1939.
(b) Gandhiji reached Rajkot in the middle of March 1939 on a peace mission.
(c) Gandhiji appealed to the Viceroy to intervene in the Rajkot struggle.
(d) None of the above.

68. The Congress Ministries, on their formation in 1937, took up for implementation the reform measures in which Gandhiji was deeply interested. In which sphere was the progress comparatively very slow, even disappointing?

(a) Basic education   (b) Prohibition
(c) Tenancy Laws   (d) Village industries

69. Subhas Chandra Bose was elected President of the Congress in 1938 with Gandhiji's goodwill. He wanted a second term, but Gandhiji did not approve of it. Despite the disapproval, Bose fought the election and won it, defeating the official candidate by over 200 votes. Gandhiji took it as a personal defeat. Identify the candidate.

   (a) Abul Kalam Azad   (b) Vallabhbhai Patel
   (c) Pattabhi Sitaramayya (d) None of the above

70. One of the resolutions proposed and adopted by the Congress in 1939 was that the President should appoint his Working Committee in consultation with Gandhiji. This was resented by the President-elect, Subhas Chandra Bose. Besides, it created a deadlock in the formation of the Working Committee. Quite many members of the old Working Committee had resigned and Gandhiji, on his part, was not prepared to suggest any names. Ultimately this led Subhas Chandra Bose to tender his resignation at the meeting of the A.I.C.C. which was called at

   (a) Tripuri   (b) Patna
   (c) Lucknow   (d) Calcutta

71. When the Second World War broke out, the British Government declared India as a belligerent country and wanted full support in its war-effort. Gandhiji, as a person, was in favour of

   (a) Unconditional support
   (b) Unconditional but only moral support
   (c) Conditional support in men, money and materials
   (d) No support at all

72. While the various left-wing groups like the Forward Block, the Congress Socialist Party and the Communist Party wanted an immediate launching of a mass struggle against British imperialism to achieve freedom, Gandhiji was against initiating any mass movement immediately after World War II broke out. What broad reason was put forward by him?

   (a) Lack of Hindu-Muslim unity which could lead to communal riots or even civil war.
   (b) The cause of the Allies being just, they should not be embarrassed in this war-effort.
   (c) Absence of favourable atmosphere in the country for an immediate struggle.
   (d) All the three.

73. As the World War II raged and the attitude of the British Government hardened and became more and more unresponsive, Gandhiji, on the command of the Congress, began to take steps which would lead to mass struggle. He worked out a limited *Satyagraha* plan on an individual basis by selected individuals. He unfolded his plan of individual *Satyagraha* or Civil Disobedience at the meeting of the Congress Working Committee held at

   (a) Bombay   (b) Wardha
   (c) Ahmedabad   (d) Lucknow

74. On which day of October 1940 was Gandhiji's Individual *Satyagraha* or Civil Disobedience Movement launched?

   (a) 25th   (b) 22nd
   (c) 17th   (d) 2nd

75. Gandhiji selected Vinoba Bhave as the first *satya-grahi* who solemnly inaugurated the Individual Civil Disobedience Movement by delivering an anti-war speech at
    (a) Pannar   (b) Kheda
    (c) Bhavnagar   (d) Rajkot

76. Who was selected by Gandhiji to follow Vinoba Bhave to offer *Satyagraha* under the Individual Civil Disobedience campaign?
    (a) J.B. Kripalani   (b) Jawaharlal Nehru
    (c) Kaka Kalelkar   (d) Devdas Gandhi

77. The main aim of the Individual Civil Disobedience Movement launched by Gandhiji in October 1941 was to
    (a) Disprove the British claim that India was voluntarily and wholeheartedly helping the war-effort.
    (b) Demand setting up of National Government immediately.
    (c) Secure full independence
    (d) Get the promise of the grant of dominion status after the end of the War.

78. As a protest against the official demand for pre-censorship of reports and writing on the subject of *satyagraha*, imposed by the Defence of India Rules, Gandhiji suspended the publication of *Harijan* and the allied weeklies. Which issue of *Harijan* was printed in bold type, bidding "good-bye" to the reader?
    (a) October 17, 1940   (b) October 24, 1940
    (c) November 10, 1940   (d) November 17, 1940

79. Towards the middle of December, 1941 the war took a menacing turn. This led the Government to expand the Viceroy's Executive Council and release most of the leaders and other Congressmen. Since majority of the Congress leaders were thinking of making a fresh cooperation in the war-effort, Gandhiji desired to be relieved of his command. The Congress Working Committee respected his wishes and relieved him of his charge at its meeting held on December 23, 1941 at

(a) Wardha   (b) Bardoli

(c) Bombay   (d) Ahmedabad

80. When India's frontiers were directly threatened, the British Government sent Sir Stafford Cripps to India with a Draft Declaration so as to secure the full cooperation of India for the overall war-effort. On his meeting in New Delhi Gandhiji found the proposals highly disappointing and rejected them. Towards the end of which month of 1942, the meeting between the two took place?

(a) January   (b) February

(c) March   (d) April

81. The Individual Civil Disobedience Movement culminated, after the failure of Cripps Mission, in the Quit India Movement of 1942. And this time again the Congress offered the leadership to Mahatma Gandhi which he readily accepted. Though Gandhiji himself had begun to talk of the coming struggle for quite some time past, the Congress Working Committee first accepted the idea of a struggle at its meeting held on July 14, 1942 at

(a) Sevagram   (b) Wardha
(c) Ahmedabad   (d) Allahabad

82. On which day of August 1942 was Gandhiji's Quit India Resolution adopted by the All-India Congress Committee?
    (a) 2nd   (b) 4th
    (c) 6th   (d) 8rh

83. The historic August session of the All-India Congress Committee, at which the Quit India Resolution was passed, was held at Gowali Park in
    (a) Bombay   (b) Ahmedabad
    (c) Lucknow   (d) Poona

84. Before the Quit India struggle could be formally launched, the Government started arresting Congress leaders on a large scale. When was Gandhiji arrested in this connection?
    (a) August 24, 1942   (b) August 15, 1942
    (c) August 12, 1942   (d) August 9, 1942

85. On being arrested for his 'Quit India' programme, where was Gandhiji detained?
    (a) Yeravda Jail   (b) Aga Khan Palace
    (c) Ahmednagar Fort (d) Ahmedabad Prison

86. In connection with the launching of which of the following did Gandhiji tell these words to Congressmen?
    "As soldiers we have to take our orders from the General and obey them implicitly. His word must be law. I am your General."
    (a) Quit India Movement
    (b) Individual Satyagraha Campaign

(c) Second Civil Disobedience Movement

(d) Dandi March

87. Whom was Gandhiji referring to when he talked about his political heir at the meeting of the A.I.C.C. held in Wardha on January 15, 1942?
    (a) Vallabhbhai Patel   (b) Rajendra Prasad
    (c) Jawaharlal Nehru   (d) Abul Kalam Azad

88. Which of the following slogans is associated with the name of Gandhiji?
    (a) Do or die
    (b) *Jai Jawan Jai Kisan*
    (c) *Swaraj* is my birth right
    (d) *Inqilab Zindabad*

89. Gandhiji began a 21-day fast on February 10, 1943 in jail which provided a burst of political activity. This fast was undertaken by him to
    (a) Condemn violence of the poeple in the Quit India Movement.
    (b) Prove his innocence before God for violence during the Quit India Movement.
    (c) Register his protest against the violence of the state, including the unwarranted detention of thousands of Congressmen.
    (d) Both (b) and (c)

90. Who of the following members of the Viceroy's Executive Council resigned when Gandhiji's February 1943 fast in jail continued and the Government remained unmoved despite mounting pressure of people from all walks of life, causing severe blow to the prestige of the Government?

(a) M.S. Aney   (b) N.R. Sarkar
(c) H.P. Mody   (d) All of the three

91. A significant feature of the Quit India Movement was the emergence of what came to be known as parallel governments in some parts of the country. The first such government was proclaimed in August 1942 under the leadership of Chittu Pandey in
(a) Ballia   (b) Gorakhpur
(c) Champaran   (d) Gaya

92. Identify the leader who published a formula on July 10, 1944 which had been discussed with as well as approved by Gandhiji and which he had sent to M.A. Jinnah in April 1944 to serve as a basis for settlement between the Congress and the Muslim League.
(a) Bhulabhai Desai   (b) C. Rajagopalachari
(c) T.B. Sapru   (d) M.R. Jayakar

93. With Gandhiji's release in May 1944, political activity in the country regained momentum. During which month in 1944 Gandhiji carried on talks with M.A. Jinnah regarding Pakistan for about three weeks which, however, did not result in any agreement?
(a) August   (b) September
(c) October   (d) November

94. The members of the Congress Working Committee were released on June 15, 1945 soon after the A.I.C.C. met in Bombay on June 21. The main business before it was to consider Lord Wavell's proposals as also his invitation to Congress leaders to meet him in conference at Simla. It authorised Gandhiji

and another leader to deal with all phases of negotiations arising out of the Simla conference. Identify the other leader.

(a) Jawaharlal Nehru   (b) Vallabhbhai Patel
(c) Abul Kalam Azad   (d) Asaf Ali

95. In which week of April 1946 was Gandhiji invited by the British Cabinet delegation, through a pressing personal message, to meet them at Delhi to discuss with them how the British could most expeditously quit India?

(a) First   (b) Second
(c) Third   (d) Fourth

96. Who of the following sent this message to Gandhiji in 1946?

"I feel the heavy burden of our present efforts and the necessity for all the help that we can have, and no help can be more welcome and wise than which you can give."

(a) Lord Wavell
(b) Lord Pethick-Lawrence
(c) Albert Alexander
(d) Sir Stafford Cripps

97. Which of the following statements is not correct?

(a) Gandhiji advised the Congress to enter Interim Government.
(b) The second phase of Gandhiji's tour through the village of Noakhali commenced in February 1947.
(c) On April 15, 1947 a communique was issued from Delhi releasing the joint appeal from Gandhiji and Qaid-e-Azam Jinnah, denouncing

for all time the use of force to achieve political ends.

(d) None of the above.

98. Identify the leader who wrote to Gandhiji in the second week of February 1947 the following words about the sickening political state in the country.

"We are drifting everywhere, and sometimes I doubt if we are drifting in the right direction. We live in a state of perpetual crisis and have no real grip of the situation."

(a) G.B. Pant   (b) Jawaharlal Nehru
(c) C. Rajagopalachari (d) Rajendra Prasad

99. Lord Mountbatten arrived in India on 22nd March 1947 as the new Viceroy in place of Lord Wavell to finalise the process of the transfer of power. His first act was to invite Gandhiji to meet him in that connection. When Gandhiji met him for the first time?

(a) March 27, 1947   (b) March 29, 1947
(c) March 31, 1947   (d) April 2, 1947

100. Gandhiji was all along strongly opposed to Partition. He regarded it as the vivisection of India. Yet circumstances so developed that he advised the members of the A.I.C.C., despite strong opposition from Purushottam Das Tandon and others, to finally accept Partition at its historic meeting held in Delhi, beginning on

(a) June 8, 1947   (b) June 10, 1947
(c) June 12, 1947   (d) June 14, 1947

101. When on August 15, 1947 the transfer of power took place, the Congress President issued a message to the nation and saluted Mahatma Gandhi as "the

maker of freedom achieved in a unique way." He said "never before was so great an event consummated with such little bloodshed and violence." Who was the Congress President?

(a) J.B. Kripalani   (b) Jawaharlal Nehru
(c) Abul Kalam Azad   (d) U.N. Dhebar

102. Gandhiji accorded very high priority to communal harmony in his programme of actions. At which place did he undertake his last fast for it on January 13, 1948?

(a) Calcutta   (b) Delhi
(c) Patna   (d) Noakhali

103. After the attainment of political independence in 1947, Gandhiji felt that the Congress, as a propaganda vehicle and a parliamentary machine, had outlived its usefulness. So to keep the Congress away from unhealthy competition with political parties and communal bodies, Gandhiji towards the end of January 1948 sketched a draft constitution for the Congress to transform itself into

(a) Gram Vikas Sanstha   (b) Sarvodaya Sangthan
(c) Lok Sevak Sangh   (d) Hind Kalyan Dal

5

Thought and Philosophy

1. After reading a particular book Gandhiji wrote:
   "I was at that time a believer in violence. Its reading cured me of my scepticism and made me a firm believer in *ahimsa*."
   Identify the book that brought about such a change in him.
   (a) *The Kingdom of God is Within You*
   (b) *India – What can it Teach Us*
   (c) *Life of Mahomed*
   (d) *The Gospel in Brief*

2. The book 'Unto This Last' greatly captivated and transformed Gandhiji. So much so that he translated it into Gujarati. Who was its author?
   (a) Rabindranath Tagore (b) John Ruskin
   (c) Leo Tolstoy   (d) Edwin Arnold

3. What title did Gandhiji give to his Gujarati translation of *Unto This Last* ?
   (a) *Harijan*   (b) *Jan Kalyan*
   (c) *Sandesh*   (d) *Sarvodaya*

4. Gandhiji's name is closely linked with *satyagraha* chiefly because
   (a) He propounded the theory of *satyagraha*.
   (b) He elaborated the theory of *satyagraha*.
   (c) He demonstrated its potentialities for the solution of individual and social problems.
   (d) Both (a) and (b)

5. Gandhiji used the term '*satyagraha*' for the first time in South Africa to indicate the movement which was originally described by him as 'passive resistance'. Later he deliberately substituted the word '*satyagraha*' for it because, according to him, passive resistance
   (a) Is a weapon of the weak.
   (b) Does not eschew violence as a matter of principle.
   (c) Has no place for love.
   (d) For all the above reasons.

6. Gandhiji laid down certain qualifications for a *satyagrahi*. Which of the following is not such a qualification?
   (a) He must believe in truth and non-violence as his creed.
   (b) He must be leading a chaste life and be ready to give up his life and possessions.
   (c) He must be able to create a fear in the wrong-doer.
   (d) He must carry out all the rules of discipline as may be laid from time to time.

7. "I have ventured to place before India the ancient law of self-sacrifice," said Gandhiji. What was he referring to?
   (a) *Satyagraha*
   (b) Non-violence
   (c) Control of desires
   (d) None of the above

8. Which of the following did Gandhiji describe as his two lungs?
   (a) Work and worship
   (b) *Ahimsa* and truth
   (c) Trust in self and love for the poor
   (d) Faith in God and abstinence from bodily pleasure

9. Gandhiji stated that "I count no sacrifice too great for the sake of seeing God face to face." How, in his own words, did he expect to achieve it?
   (a) By serving the country and working for its freedom
   (b) By serving the lowliest of God's creatures
   (c) By struggling to reach the status of the lowliest of His creatures
   (d) By fasting and reading scriptures regularly

10. Which of the following, according to Gandhiji, is an essential principle of *satyagraha*?
    (a) Truth
    (b) Non-violence
    (c) Purity of means
    (d) All the three

11. Which one of the following did Gandhiji exhort his countrymen to follow as a gospel?
    (a) Patriotism
    (b) Self-sacrifice
    (c) Humility
    (d) Communal harmony

12. Gandhiji considered one of the following as the only source of his strength. Which was that?
    (a) Faith in God
    (b) Belief in truth
    (c) Consciousness of his limitations
    (d) Practice of *ahimsa*

13. Fill in the blank with one of the following words to complete the statement of Gandhiji that "I am anxious, indeed I am impatient to demonstrate that there is no remedy for the many ills in life save that of _____."
    (a) Non-violence   (b) Truthfulness
    (c) Patience   (d) Godliness

14. Which of the following expressions Gandhiji ultimately found it more accurate?
    (a) God is Truth   (b) Truth is God
    (c) God is Light   (d) God is Love

15. Identify the incorrect statement about a *satyagrahi* from the Gandhian view-point.
    (a) He must be fearless.
    (b) His object is never to coerce the wrong-doer.
    (c) He must welcome honourable opportunity for peace.
    (d) None of the above.

16. Gandhiji said about some people that "They will call you and me friends if we talk about God to them. They know, if they know any God at all, a God of terror, vengeance, a pitiless tyrant." Who are these people he is referring to?
    (a) The poor   (b) The capitalists
    (c) The terrorists   (d) The wrong-doers

17. Given below are some observations on religion and politics. Identify the one which is not Gandhiji's observation.
    (a) "Those who say that religion has nothing to do with politics do not know what religion means."
    (b) "If any one told me that God was a god of untruth or a god of torture, I would continue to worship him."
    (c) "Religion is no test of nationality, but a personal matter between man and his God."
    (d) "My politics and all activities of mine are derived from my religion."

18. Which of the following is the viewpoint of Gandhiji?
    (a) "Hinduism is not an exclusive religion. In it there is room for worship of all prophets in the world."
    (b) "The Gita is not only my Bible or my Koran; it is much more than that – it is my mother."
    (c) "It is my firm opinion that Europe today represents not the spirit of God or Christianity, but the spirit of Satan."
    (d) All the above

19. Gandhiji considered one of the following as the farthest limit of humility. Identify it.
    (a) *Ahimsa*   (b) Truth
    (c) Labour for the poor (d) None of the above

20. Gandhiji wrote in *Young India* in 1925: "Do not seek to protect me." Which of the following was the source of this view of Gandhiji?
    (a) He was aching for martyrdom.
    (b) He was angry for assaults made on his life.

(c) God saves all life according to His will.

(d) None of the above.

21. Gandhiji described his insistence on the personality traits as "my all." Which of the following is not a part of these traits?

(a) Non-violence   (b) Truth

(c) *Brahmacharya*   (d) Mahatmaship

22. Gandhiji stated that "I do not give vent to anger." Which of the following was the reason for it?

(a) He wanted to control his anger to transmit it into a power over man and matter.

(b) He was tolerant of others who deviated from code of honour.

(c) He did not get angry.

(d) Both (b) and (c)

23. A firm believer in the principle of *satyagraha*, Gandhiji was strongly opposed to sitting on '*dharna*' because

(a) It is a crude way of using coercion.

(b) It is cowardly.

(c) It is worse than violence.

(d) For all the three reasons.

24. What was Gandhiji's motive as a living being?

(a) To be counted among one of the prophets.

(b) To do social service.

(c) To free his soul from the bondage of flesh.

(d) To live a long and healthy life.

25. Gandhiji believed that there is a possibility of harm to one's cause by outside agencies only under some

circumstances. Which of the following is not one of these circumstances?

(a) Cause is bad.
(b) Champions of the cause are untrue.
(c) Champions of the cause lack courage.
(d) Champions of the cause are physically weak.

26. What was the highest honour that Gandhiji expected from his friends or followers?
    (a) To promote the activities that he stood for.
    (b) To resist him to their utmost if they did not believe in his programme.
    (c) Both (a) and (b)
    (d) To propogate his philosophy.

27. Gandhiji described himself as a "seeker after truth" and he claimed that
    (a) He had found it.
    (b) He had found a way to it.
    (c) He was making a ceaseless effort to it.
    (d) Both (b) and (c)

28. Fasting is a potent weapon in the armoury of *satyagraha*. Which of the following is not the observation of Gandhiji on fasting?
    (a) Physical capacity to undertake fast is a necessary qualification for it.
    (b) One should fast only as a last resort where all other avenues of redress have been explored and have failed.
    (c) Fasting is a spiritual act and is, therfore, addressed to God.

(d) It cannot be undertaken mechanically. It is a powerful thing but a dangerous thing if handled amateurishly.

29. Gandhiji made some observations about non-violent way and his practice of it. Which of the following is not one such observation?
   (a) "God has given me the power to guide the world on the path of non-violence."
   (b) "God has chosen me as his instrument for presenting non-violence to India for dealing with her many ills."
   (c) "I should ... rise, even if I was alone, against the methods of actual violence."
   (d) "My non-violence does not admit of running away from danger and leaving dear ones unprotected. Between violence and cowardly flight, I can prefer violence to cowardice."

30. Gandhiji disapproved of flattery. Which was, according to him, the form of sincerest flattery?
   (a) Stating adjectives at one's back.
   (b) Imitation of the qualities.
   (c) Stating truth about a person's qualities on his face.
   (d) Talking about personal qualities by oneself.

31. Which of the following observations in respect of training for non-violence represents the viewpoint of Gandhiji?
   (a) Non-violence does not require any outward training.
   (b) Non-violence cannot be learnt by staying at home; it needs enterprise.

(c) Both (a) and (b)

(d) It is essential to learn violence before we can learn non-violence.

32. Gandhiji made a distinction between passive resistance and non-violence. What was the distinction?

(a) Passive resistance is the resistance offered by the weak because they are unable to offer armed resistance, whereas non-violence is the resistance offered by the strong because they are unwilling to offer armed resistance.

(b) Passive resistance is the resistance offered by *satyagrahis* in the form of fasts and vows of silence, whereas non-violence stands for not raising armed resistance in the face of state violence.

(c) Passive resistance means strikes and closing down of work establishments, whereas non-violence means demonstrations and other allied activities where work is not stopped.

(d) All of the above.

33. Which of the following is not Gandhiji's view about women?

(a) They are more self-sacrificing than men.

(b) They have greater courage than men.

(c) They are the weaker sex.

(d) Both (a) and (b)

34. What did Gandhiji suggest to the Indian women to enable them to realise their potential?

(a) They have to be the complement of man.

(b) They must do whatever men can do.

(c) They must organise themselves to assert their rights.

(d) They should follow the Western women in their behaviour towards social issues.

35. According to Gandhiji vocations of men and women must be different. What argument did he give for it?
    (a) Women are the weaker sex.
    (b) Women are incapable of performing certain activities.
    (c) Women cannot do many things without men's help.
    (d) There is a vital difference in form.

36. Gandhiji advised women to become fearless and brave to protect their honour. They can become so, according to him, through
    (a) Living faith in God
    (b) Acquiring adequate physical strength
    (c) Special training
    (d) Both (b) and (c)

37. In which respect Gandhiji held woman as man's superior?
    (a) Self-sacrifice
    (b) Moral power
    (c) *Ahimsa*
    (d) All of the above

38. What is, according to Gandhiji, the most effective defence of a woman against physical assault to outrage her modesty?
    (a) Full physical strength, including weapons of violence, used in self-defence against the assailant.

(b) Strength of the woman's purity and determination to lay down her life rather than allow the assailant to overpower her.

(c) Exemplary and prompt judicial punishment of the assailant as a deterrent to prospective assailants.

(d) Social boycott of the assailant, including his family and friends.

39. Gandhiji regarded marriage as a sacrament. It could be seen to involve
    (a) Mutual consent   (b) Self-control
    (c) Mutual love   (d) All the above

40. Which of the following was regarded by Gandhiji as the proper method of dealing with brothels?
    (a) Propaganda amongst women who sell their honour for a livelihood.
    (b) Propaganda amongst men who visit brothels.
    (c) Both (a) and (b)
    (d) Enacting suitable legislation to declare prostitution illegal.

41. Who, according to Gandhiji, are best suited to impart sex education to children?
    (a) Parents of children who can freely tell them do's and do'nts of sex.
    (b) Specialist teachers of the science of sex-control who have acquired mastery over self.
    (c) Religious preachers who should be invited to impart such education in schools.
    (d) Teachers who teach biological sciences.

42. Which of the following is a close approximation to Gandhiji's views on sex education?

(a) It is necessary to impart to young pupils a knowledge about the use and function of generative organs to a certain extent.

(b) The objective of sex education must be the conquest and sublimation of sex passion.

(c) Both (a) and (b)

(d) Imparting such education will only weaken the moral fabric of society.

43. Gandhiji emphasised that life without *brahmachrya* would be animal-like. For *brahmacharya* he accorded primacy to control one of the following. Identify it.

(a) Thought   (b) Sense

(c) Word   (d) Deed

44. Gandhiji advocated birth-control through the practice of *brahmacharya* for the sake of

(a) Prevention of increase in population.

(b) Improvement in the quality of human beings.

(c) Avoiding the birth of unwanted children.

(d) All of the above.

45. Which of the following is not Gandhiji's view in respect of *brahmacharya* or its practice?

(a) It is a virtue that can be cultivated by outward restraints.

(b) It is a mental condition.

(c) Mere control of animal passion is an incomplete and wrong concept of *brahmacharya*.

(d) It must be observed in thought, word and deed.

46. Gandhiji did not approve the use of artificial means of birth-control because he felt that

(a) Sexual union is meant only for procreation.

   (b) Artificial methods would put a premium on vice.

   (c) Self-control on *brahmacharya* is a remedy that does good to those who practice it.

   (d) All of the above.

47. Which of the following sums up Gandhiji's view on the use of contraceptives?
   (a) A necessary evil.
   (b) A tool whose use should be strictly limited to married men and women only.
   (c) Both (a) and (b)
   (d) An insult to womanhood.

48. Gandhiji was against widowhood imposed by religion or custom. What reason did he give for it?
   (a) it is an unbearable yoke.
   (b) It defies the home by secret vice.
   (c) It degrades religion.
   (d) All the three.

49. Gandhiji stated in 1947: "If untouchability lives, Hinduism must die." When did he start questioning the scourge of untouchability?
   (a) Early in his boyhood
   (b) During his stay in London
   (c) Soon after reaching South Africa
   (d) On his return to India from South Africa

50. What is, according to Gandhiji, the main obstacle in the way of social reform in India?
   (a) Inadequacy of financial support
   (b) Absence of people's interest
   (c) Want of genuine social reformers
   (d) Lack of legal support

51. Which one of the following was regarded by Gandhiji as an essential pre-requisite for a good public worker?
    (a) Character
    (b) Hard work
    (c) Opinion leadership
    (d) General acceptability

52. Cow protection to Gandhiji was one of the most wonderful phenomena in human evolution, and he regarded it as the gift of Hinduism to the world. He drew up a list of main measures for the protection of cows. Which of the following is not one such measure?
    (a) Learning the science of cattle breeding
    (b) Hindus performing their duty towards the cow and her progeny
    (c) Thorough reform of *pingrapoles* (institutions for aged cows)
    (d) Legislation to ban cow-slaughter

53. Which of the following did Gandhiji consider as the noblest activity of man?
    (a) Working for communal harmony
    (b) Doing the labour that poor must do
    (c) Performing national service
    (d) Reading spiritual books for some time every day

54. Gandhiji adopted a principle of 'bread labour'. What was it?
    (a) Earnings of every person must be no more or no less than the price of bread needed to sustain him.

(b) Labour working in the agricultural sector.
(c) Every man must labour with his body for his food and clothing.
(d) Labour engaged in social services.

55. Which of the following is inconsistent with the Gandhian thought in respect of physical and intellectual labour?
    (a) Mere intellectual labour is for the soul and is its own satisfaction. It should never demand payment.
    (b) No man ought to be free from the obligation of doing physical labour.
    (c) No amount of intellectual labour is any compensation for bodily labour.
    (d) None of the above.

56. Which of the following is inconsistent with the Gandhiji's views on labour?
    (a) Labour discharges its obligations more effectively and conscientiously than the employer.
    (b) Labour must seize capital and become capitalist itself.
    (c) Labour can always vindicate itself if it is adequately united and is willing to make any sacrifice.
    (d) Those who take their wages without doing the allotted work indulge in theft.

57. Gandhiji made some observations about the interrelationship between rights and duties. Which of the following would you attribute to him?
    (a) Right to perform one's duties is the only right that is worth living for and dying for.

(b) True source of right is duty.

(c) Rights are independent of duties.

(d) Both (a) and (b)

58. Identify the Gandhian method of ending capitalist's exploitation of labour.

(a) Destruction of the capitalist.

(b) All capital to be taken over by the state and private ownership be abolished.

(c) Labour to cooperate with the capitalists so as to maximize production.

(d) Labour to adopt non-cooperation as a weapon to convert its exploiters.

59. Gandhiji regarded certain conditions as pre-requisites for a successful strike. Which of the following is not one such condition?

(a) The cause of the strike must be political and involve most workers.

(b) The cause of the strike must be just.

(c) There should be near unanimity among the strikers.

(d) The strikers should not be dependent upon the union funds for their sustenance during the strike period.

60. Which of the following is consistent with Gandhiji's views on strikes by labour?

(a) Strikes should take place only for the direct improvement of workers' condition.

(b) Strikes, which are also designed to serve political ends, are a form of non-violent non-cooperation.

    (c) Strikes can be legitimately used by Indian labour for attaining political objectives.

    (d) The greatest political contribution that labourers can make is to join strikes for regulating the functioning of the state.

61. Gandhiji made several observations about the modern machines. Which of the following is not one such observation?
    (a) "I would not weep over the disappearance of machinery or consider it a calamity."
    (b) "The machine should not tend to make atrophied the limbs of man."
    (c) "Due to the achievements of the machine age, handicrafts will ultimately disappear."
    (d) "Machinery is like a snake-hole which may contain one to a hundred snakes."

62. Gandhiji was uncompromisingly against all "destructive machinery". What did he mean by "destructive machinery"?
    (a) Machinery which displaces labour and leaves it idle.
    (b) Machines which are used to produce arsenal and other chemical weapons.
    (c) Machinery which is used to produce liquor and other intoxicants.
    (d) Both (b) and (c)

63. Gandhiji said that "Dead machinery must not be pitted against the millions of living machines." What did he mean by living machines?
    (a) Simple tools and implements used by artisans and other workers.

(b) Artisans and workers scattered over the land.
(c) Machines which consume a whole lot of fuel and energy.
(d) Machines used in laboratories to develop new technology.

64. Which of the following observations on industrialism was made by Gandhiji?
(a) The future of industrialism is dark.
(b) Industrialism thrives on the exploitation of others.
(c) God forbid that India should ever take industrialism after the manner of the West.
(d) All of the above.

65. Identify the incorrect statement.
Gandhiji was against
(a) Development of science and technology.
(b) All mechanised big industry.
(c) Both (a) and (b)
(d) Multiplication of wants.

66. Which of the following measures was suggested by Gandhiji to improve the conditions of the Indian peasants?
(a) *Zamindari* should be abolished by legislation.
(b) *Zamindars* should be forced to surrender their surplus land by imposing ceiling on land holdings and the surplus land be distributed among the landless.
(c) Peasants must be protected against exploitation by fixing minimum wages for them.

(d) *Zamindars* should be induced to share their riches and voluntarily surrender their superfluous acquisitions to the masses.

67. In the following statement by Gandhiji fill in the blank with appropriate word from among the words given below.
"Even as the _____ is India's comforter today, it may even be world's tomorrow, because it stands not for the greatest number, but for the greatest good for all."
(a) *Charkha*
(b) Non-violence
(c) Limitation of wants
(d) *Satyagraha*

68. Which of the following closely reflects Gandhiji's view on honesty in business?
(a) It is impossible for a businessman to conduct strictly honest business.
(b) It is difficult for a businessman to conduct strictly honest business.
(c) Honesty makes unbearable demands on the resources of a businessman.
(d) An honest businessman will be somewhat less successful.

69. Which of the following is inconsistent with the Gandhian economic thought?
(a) Economic equality implies that everyone will have the same amount.
(b) The real meaning of equality is "To each according to his needs".
(c) Accumulation of capital by private persons is impossible except through violent means.

111

(d) Accumulation by the state in a non-violent society is not only possible, it is desirable and inevitable.

70. Gandhiji suggested several steps for bringing about equitable distribution in society. Which of the following is consistent with his way of thinking?
   (a) The programme of equitable distribution should be propagated and canvassed for more and more adherants.
   (b) The ideal of equitable distribution need not begin at the level of the whole society. Even one individual can give it a start by reducing his wants to a minimum.
   (c) To promote the ideal, the best methods of production should be adopted.
   (d) The wealthy should follow the ideal first and thus give a lead.

71. Which of the following is inconsistent with the Gandhian Theory of Trusteeship?
   (a) An upper limit to income and a minimum decent living wage should be fixed. The difference between the two should be reasonable and variable from time to time so much so that the tendency would be towards obliteration of the difference.
   (b) It provides a means of transforming the present capitalist order of society into an equalitarian one.
   (c) It excludes legislative regulation of the ownership and use of wealth.
   (d) The character of production will be determined by social necessity.

72. What was Gandhiji's solution to a failure of the rich to voluntarily accept trusteeship as a means of managing economic activity?
    (a) Planning
    (b) Non-violent cooperation
    (c) Nationalisation of property
    (d) *Panchayati Raj*

73. How did Gandhiji look upon secrecy in politics?
    (a) A necessary evil
    (b) A diplomatic necessity
    (c) A sin
    (d) A desirable instrument for achieving goals

74. Gandhiji had placed freedom on a high pedestal. Some of his observations on freedom are among the following. Identify the one which is not Gandhiji's view of freedom.
    (a) Freedom is not worth having if it does not connote freedom to err and even to sin.
    (b) No man loses his freedom except through his own weakness.
    (c) Freedom is like a birth. Till we are fully free, we are slaves.
    (d) Individual freedom is the law of the beast of the jungle.

75. "In concrete terms ... the independence should be political, economic and moral," said Gandhiji. What was his view of moral independence?
    (a) Freedom from armed defence forces.
    (b) Freedom from communal divisions.

(c) Freedom from antagonism between the rich and the poor.

(d) Freedom from caste rigidities.

76. What was Gandhiji's concept of freedom?
   (a) It is co-extensive with the freedom of man in all his majesty.
   (b) Freedom is never at any price.
   (c) Man has to thank himself for his dependence. He can be independent as soon as he wills it.
   (d) All the above.

77. What did Gandhiji mean by "*Swaraj*"?
   (a) Freedom from all restraint.
   (b) Freedom for the meanest of the countrymen.
   (c) Rule of the majority.
   (d) Freedom from foreign yoke.

78. Which of the following represents Gandhiji's view on the achievement of *swaraj* ?
   (a) *Swaraj* can never be a free gift by one nation to another. It is a treasure to be purchased with a nation's best blood.
   (b) Progress towards *swaraj* will be in exact proportion to the increase in the number of determined workers who will dare to sacrifice their all for the casue of the poor.
   (c) Both (a) and (b)
   (d) To achieve *swaraj*, there is the need for deliberate creation of anarchical state to overthrow the established order in the hope of throwing up from within a dictator who would rule with a rod of iron and produce order out of disorder.

79. According to Gandhiji 'Poorna Swaraj' refers to a state where
   (a) The necessaries of life are equally enjoyed by the rich and the poor.
   (b) There is a progressive improvement in the economic conditions of the masses.
   (c) Both (a) and (b).
   (d) The poor enjoy all the luxuries which the princes and the moneyed people enjoyed before freedom.

80. What did Gandhiji broadly mean by 'Ramrajya'?
   (a) Replacement of the British army by a national army.
   (b) Sovereignty of the people based on pure moral authority.
   (c) Establishment of rule by the majority.
   (d) System similar to erstwhile Soviet rule of Russia.

81. Identify the incorrect statement.
   (a) Gandhiji was not anti-British.
   (b) Gandhiji observed that politics, divorced from religion, has absolutely no meaning.
   (c) "We must be content to die," said Gandhiji, "if we cannot live as free men and women."
   (d) Gandhiji believed that world peace could be achieved through a policy of balance of power.

82. Which of the following constitutes the primary points of difference between socialism of Western conception and the Gandhian view of socialism.
   (a) Material progress without violence.

(b) Equality of all mankind irrespective of the material wealth.

(c) State ownership of all means of production without violence.

(d) First control of the state to be followed by enforcement of equality by law.

83. Which of the following statements in respect of the Indian National Congress can be attributed to Gandhiji?

(a) The Congress will die a natural and deserved death if and when it substitutes reason and moral influence by *goondaism*.

(b) If the heads of the Congress committees are indifferent or supine, the corruption cannot be dealt with.

(c) With the advent of power, the Congressmen have begun to think that everything belongs to them.

(d) All the above.

84. What is, according to Gandhiji, the true function of journalism?

(a) Provide facts to stock the public mind with wanted facts.

(b) Educate the public mind.

(c) Leading opinion of the public towards certain pre-determined ends.

(d) All the above.

85. Which of the following is the view of Gandhiji in respect of profession of lawyers?

(a) It is not impossible to practise law without making it subservient to the interest of the lawyer's purse.

(b) It is the duty of a lawyer to defend even if the lawyer knows him to be guilty.

(c) It is impossible to practise law without compromising truth.

(d) True function of a lawyer is to induce people to seek justice from the court of law.

86. Identify the view of Gandhiji on jury trials.
    (a) Jury trials are always on the side of leniency.
    (b) Jury trials are always better than those by judges.
    (c) At the right moment jury has been found to fail.
    (d) As an institution of justice, it needs to be copied from England.

87. Below are given some observations on newspapers and truth. Identify the observation made by Gandhiji.
    (a) All that appears in newspapers is looked upon as God's truth.
    (b) It is the duty of newspapers to give nothing but facts to their readers.
    (c) The habit of borrowing opinions from newspapers is to be deprecated.
    (d) All of the above.

88. Identify the Gandhian view of morality.
    (a) Morality consists in finding the true path for ourselves and in fearlessly following it.
    (b) No action which is not voluntary can be called moral.

(c) Both (a) and (b).
(d) Moral authority can be retained by an attempt to hold on to it.

89. Which of the following is a close approximation to the Gandhian view of the purchase of 'swadeshi'?
   (a) A villager buying goods manufactured in his country.
   (b) A villager buying goods produced in his village.
   (c) A villager buying goods manufactured by the traditional technology of the country in his own country.
   (d) A villager buying goods manufactured by his countrymen anywhere in the world.

90. Which of the following represents Gandhiji's view on smoking?
   (a) Smoking is a curse next only to drinking.
   (b) Chewing tobacco may be excused because it has some advantages.
   (c) Smoking is an expensive vice.
   (d) Both (a) and (b).

91. Which of the following statements about Gandhiji and education is incorrect?
   (a) He was against the creation of states on a linguistic basis.
   (b) His *Nai Talim* was a beautiful blend of craft, art, health and education and covered the whole education of the individual from the time of birth to the moment of death.
   (c) His scheme was designed to be wholly self-supporting.

(d) The inter-state language can only be Hindustani written in Nagari or Urdu script.

92. Which of the following, in general, was not favoured by Gandhiji?
    (a) Ban on cow-slaughter
    (b) Western medical treatment
    (c) *Sadavrat* i.e. free kitchen for the poor
    (d) All the three

93. Identify the statement which is not in tune with the Gandhian viewpoint.
    (a) To call woman the weaker sex is a libel; it is man's injustice to woman.
    (b) Gandhiji was a believer in previous births and rebirths.
    (c) He believed in inherited riches
    (d) According to Gandhiji, money is the last thing that a social reformer needs in his campaign.

6

Literature

Gandhiji's *The Story of My Experiments with Truth* was originally written in Gujarati. Who translated it into English?
(a) V.G. Desai   (b) Mahadev Desai
(c) Sushila Nayar   (') Pyarelal

2. Which one of the following books is the work of Gandhiji?
   (a) *The Gospel of Swadeshi*
   (b) *Ethical Religion*
   (c) *The India of My Dreams*
   (d) Both (b) and (c)

3. Gandhiji brought his *Autography* upto
   (a) 1920   (b) 1925
   (c) 1928   (d) 1930

4. Identify the author of *Gandhi, A Study in Revolution*.
   (a) Louis Fischer   (b) Geoffrey Ashe
   (c) S.K. George   (d) N.K. Bose

5. Who wrote *Mahatmaji and the Depressed Humanity*?

(a) D.G. Tendulkar   (b) S. Radhakrishnan
(c) Rabindranath Tagore (d) C.F. Andrews

6. Which of the following is the work of C.F. Andrews?
   (a) *Mahatma Gandhi at Work*
   (b) *Glimpses of Gandhiji*
   (c) *My Days With Gandhi*
   (d) *None of the above*

7. Who is the author of *The Epic Fast*?
   (a) K.G. Mashruwala   (b) Pyarelal
   (c) J.C. Kumarappa   (d) N.K. Bose

8. Identify the author of *Mahatma Gandhi: A Biography*.
   (a) Krishna Kripalani   (b) P.C. Ghosh
   (c) Kaka Kalelkar   (d) B.R. Nanda

9. Who translated into English *Satyagraha in South Africa* by M.K. Gandhi?
   (a) V.G. Desai   (b) Manubhai Gandhi
   (c) Sushila Nayar   (d) Mahadev Desai

10. Which of the following works on Gandhiji was brought out by the All-India Congress Committee in 1935?
    (a) *Satyagraha in Gandhi's Own Words*
    (b) *Satyagraha — its Technique and History*
    (c) *Mahatma Gandhi's Ideas*
    (d) *War Without Violence*

11. *Women and Social Injustice* by M.K. Gandhi was published by Navjivan Publishing House, Ahmedabad originally in

(a) 1939   (b) 1942
(c) 1944   (d) 1946

12. Identify the author of *Mahatma Gandhi and the Modern World*.
    (a) Louis Fischer   (b) Amiya Chakravarty
    (c) C.F. Andrews   (d) R.K. Prabhu

13. Who is the author of *The Philosophy of Mahatma Gandhi* ?
    (a) S.N. Dasgupta
    (b) John Hick
    (c) S. Radhakrishnan
    (d) Dhirendra Mohan Datta

14. Identify the author of *Metaphysical Foundations of Mahatma Gandhi's Thoughts*.
    (a) Surendra Verma   (b) L.C. Sharma
    (c) T.R. Mahadevan   (d) P.N. Rao

15. Gandhiji's booklet *Hind Swaraj* is a severe condemnation of modern civilisation. When was it written?
    (a) 1907   (b) 1909
    (c) 1911   (d) 1913

16. In respect of which of the following books Gandhiji used the question-answer format?
    (a) *Glances at Islam*
    (b) *Hind Swaraj*
    (c) *Cent Per Cent Swadeshi*
    (d) *Key to Health*

17. Who is the author of *Mahatma Gandhi: A Great Life in Brief* ?

(a) Vincent Sheean   (b) Morarji Desai
(c) G. Ramachandran   (d) Vinoba Bhave

18. Who wrote *Stray Glimpses of Bapu*?
    (a) Prabhudas Gandhi   (b) N.K. Bose
    (c) Kaka Kalelkar   (d) Pyarelal

19. Identify the author of *The Gandhian Alternative to Western Socialism*.
    (a) S. Dasgupta   (b) V.K.R.V. Rao
    (c) Raj Krishna   (d) N.M. Vyas

20. Identify the author of *Mahatma: Life of Mohandas Karamchand Gandhi*.
    (a) R.K. Prabhu   (b) J.B. Kripalani
    (c) D.G. Tendulkar   (d) R.R. Diwakar

21. How many volumes of *Mahatma: Life of Mohandas Karamchand Gandhi* have been published?
    (a) Five   (b) Six
    (c) Seven   (d) Eight

22. Who wrote *Bapu – My Mother* ?
    (a) Sushila Nayar   (b) Manubehn Gandhi
    (c) A. Kaur   (d) None of the above

23. During his incarceration in 1930 in the Yeravda Central Prison, Gandhiji wrote weekly letters to the Satyagraha Ashram, containing a cursory examination of the principal Ashram observances. These were later published in the form of a booklet *From Yeravda Mandir*. How many such letters does this booklet contain?
    (a) Twelve   (b) Fourteen
    (c) Sixteen   (d) Eighteen

24. Which of the following works on Gandhiji has been edited by C.F. Andrews
    (a) *Mahatma Gandhi at Work*
    (b) *Mahatma Gandhi: His Own Story*
    (c) *Mahatma Gandhi's Ideas*
    (d) All of the above

25. Identify the author of *My Days with Gandhi*.
    (a) Vinoba Bhave   (b) N.K. Bose
    (c) K.G. Mashruwala   (d) Manubhai Gandhi

26. Which of the following books on Gandhiji is the work of Pyarelal
    (a) *A Nation Builder at Work*
    (b) *Gandhian Techniques in the Modern World*
    (c) *Towards New Horizons*
    (d) All the three

27. *Satyagraha in South Africa* by M.K. Gandhi is dedicated to
    (a) G.K. .Gokhale   (b) Maganlal Gandhi
    (c) C.F. Andrews   (d) H.S.L. Polak

28. Written primarily for the teenagers, *Bahuroopee Gandhi* carries a Foreword by Jawaharlal Nehru. Who wrote it?
    (a) Anu Bandopadhyaya (b) P.R. Sen
    (c) M. Chalpathi Rau   (d) Kaka Kalelkar

29. Identify the work of Prabhudas Gandhi.
    (a) *Gandhi: Warrior of Non-Violence*
    (b) *Anecdotes from Bapu's Life*
    (c) *My Childhood with Gandhiji*
    (d) None of the above

30. Identify the author of *My Memorable Moments with Bapu*.
    - (a) Louis Fischer
    - (b) Manubehn Gandhi
    - (c) P.D. Tandon
    - (d) G.D. Birla

31. *Contemporary Crisis and Gandhi* has been edited by
    - (a) Raghvan Iyer
    - (b) S.R. Bakshi
    - (c) Ramashray Roy
    - (d) Vinit Haksar

32. Who is the author of *Gandhi's Emissary*
    - (a) N.K. Bose
    - (b) G.D. Birla
    - (c) Mahadev Desai
    - (d) Sudhir Ghosh

33. Who wrote *The Political Philosophy of Mahatma Gandhi* ?
    - (a) G.N. Dhawan
    - (b) N.K. Bose
    - (c) R.K. Prabhu
    - (d) J.B. Kripalani

34. Identify the author of *Marx and Gandhi*.
    - (a) U.R. Rao
    - (b) M. Dandavate
    - (c) Robert Hart
    - (d) Romesh Thapar

35. *Adhunik Sandarbh Mein Gandhi Vichar* has been edited by
    - (a) B.P. Sinha
    - (b) S.R. Gupta
    - (c) B.K. Lal
    - (d) S.N. Agrawal

36. Who is the author of *The Moral and Political Thought of Mahatma Gandhi*, published by Oxford University Press, New York?
    - (a) P. Nagaraja Rao
    - (b) Raghvan Iyer
    - (c) Paul F. Power
    - (d) S. Radhakrishnan

37. Which of the following is the work of B.N. Ganguli?
    - (a) *Gandhi's Social philosophy — Perspective and Relevance*

    (b) *Gandhian Outlook and Techniques*
    (c) *Gandhian Economics*
    (d) *Economics of Khaddar*

38. When did Gandhiji write the famous *Green Pamphlet?*
    (a) 1906   (b) 1904
    (c) 1896   (d) 1894

39. Identify the author of *Selections from Gandhi*, published by Navjivan Publishing House.
    (a) Mahadev Desai   (b) S.K. George
    (c) Chandra Kumar   (d) N.K. Bose

40. Who is the author of *Gandhism Reconsidered* ?
    (a) R. Coupland   (b) M.L. Dantwala
    (c) S.A. Dange   (d) N.N. Dasgupta

41. *In the Shadow of Mahatma* is the work of
    (a) G.D. Birla   (b) Annie Besant
    (c) Gopinath Dhawan (d) Mahadev Desai

42. Which of the following 'book and author' combinations is incorrect?
    (a) *Gandhi on World Affairs* — F. Paul Power
    (b) *What Does Gandhi Want* — T.A. Raman
    (c) *Gandhi vs. Lenin* — P.C. Ghosh
    (d) *On Tour with Gandhi* — B. Kumarappa

43. *Bapu: A Unique Association* contains correspondence of Gandhiji and G.D. Birla which runs into four volumes, each nearly 500 pages. When was it published?
    (a) 1985   (b) 1977
    (c) 1967   (d) 1956

44. Identify the author of *Thoreau, Tolstoy and Gandhi*.
   - (a) H.M. Vyas
   - (b) Pyarelal
   - (c) N. Prasad
   - (d) P.N. Rao

45. Who is the author of *Foundations of Gandhian Economics* ?
   - (a) J.K. Mehta
   - (b) B.N. Ganguli
   - (c) Amritananda Das
   - (d) C.N. Vakil

46. *Tolstoy and Gandhi* is the work of
   - (a) C. Shankaran Nair
   - (b) Kalidas Nag
   - (c) N.N. Mitra
   - (d) S. Mahadevan

47. Who is the editor of *Problems and Issues in Gandhism*?
   - (a) V.T. Patel
   - (b) J.S. Mathur
   - (c) B.K. Mishra
   - (d) K.C. Chacko

48. *All Men are Brothers* deals with the life and thoughts of Mahatma Gandhi as told in his own words. Who compiled and edited it?
   - (a) Rajendra Prasad
   - (b) Krishna Kripalani
   - (c) B. Kumarappa
   - (d) G.D. Birla

49. Which of the following books relating to Gandhiji has been written by Rajendra Prasad?
   - (a) *Gandhiji in Champaran*
   - (b) *Mahatma Gandhi in Bihar*
   - (c) *Constructive Programme*
   - (d) All of the above

50. Identify the author of *Gandhi As I Know Him* ?
   - (a) Pyarelal
   - (b) Indulal K. Yagnik
   - (c) Kaka Kalelkar
   - (d) B. Kumarappa

51. *Thus Spake Bapu* is the work of

(a) Pran Chopra   (b) Abid Hussain
(c) Nageshwar Prasad (d) M.L. Gujral

52. Which of the following is the work of Homer A. Jack?
    (a) *The Gandhi Reader*
    (b) *The Wit and Wisdom of Gandhi*
    (c) *Life of Mahatma Gandhi*
    (d) Both (a) and (b)

53. Which of the following books on Gandhiji has been written by Jawaharlal Nehru?
    (a) *Bapu Meri Nazar Mein*
    (b) *Freedom from Fear*
    (c) Both (a) and (b)
    (d) *Aaj Ke Sawal: Gandhi Ke Jawab*

54. Identify the author of *Gandhi, Marx and India*.
    (a) S.S. Gangal   (b) Pradhan S. Prasad
    (c) S. Dasgupta   (d) S.A. Dange

55. Who is the author of *Gandhi and Non-Cooperation Movement* ?
    (a) Nand Kishore Singh (b) M. Dandavate
    (c) P.C. Ghosh   (d) N.K. Bose

56. *Gandhi – Prisoner of Hope* is the work of
    (a) Louis Fischer   (b) J.M. Brown
    (c) H.S.L. Polak   (d) S.R. Bakshi

57. Dealing mainly with the events leading to the South African Indian *Satyagraha*, *My Childhood with Gandhiji* helps to record the creative period in Gandhiji's life which ultimately led to the major test

of building up the great movement of Indian independence. Identify its author.
(a) Prabhudas Gandhi   (b) Kaka Kalelkar
(c) Vinoba Bhave   (d) Maganlal Gandhi

58. *Anecdotes from Bapu's Life* has been compiled by
(a) Pyarelal   (b) Gurdial Mallik
(c) Mukulbhai Kalarthe   (d) D.G. Tendulkar

59. *Constructive Programme*, a booklet of 25 pages, dealing with its meaning and role in the achievement of non-violent independence, was written by Gandhiji in the train while travelling from Sevagram to
(a) Bardoli   (b) Delhi
(c) Nagpur   (d) Bhopal

60. Identify the author of *Gandhi: His Life and Thought*
(a) J.B. Kripalani   (b) S. Radhakrishnan
(c) R.R. Diwakar   (d) Louis Fischer

61. *Gandhi's Truth* has been published by Faber and Faber, London. Who is its author?
(a) J.R. Jones   (b) John E. Smith
(c) Erik H. Erikson   (d) N.K. Bose

62. When did Gandhiji start the publication of a weekly paper, *Harijan*, to promote the anti-untouchability campaign?
(a) 1935   (b) 1933
(c) 1931   (d) 1930

63. Identify the author of *Exploring Gandhi*.

(a) R.R. Diwakar
(b) J.B. Kripalani
(c) Manmohan Choudhari
(d) Suresh Ram

64. Who has written *Bapu ki Karavas Kahani* ?
(a) P.D. Tandon   (b) Sushila Nayar
(c) Pyarelal   (d) Kaka Kalelkar

65. Who wrote the editorial note to *Gandhi's Collected Writings on Non-Violent Resistance* ?
(a) Bharatan Kumarappa   (b) Morarji Desai
(c) S. Radhakrishnan   (d) R.R. Diwakar

66. *Gandhi on Women* is the work of
(a) Sucheta Kripalani   (b) Sushila Nayar
(c) Mirabehn   (d) Pushpa Joshi

67. The book *Pilgrim Centenary: A Rememberance* gives a good critical account of the observance of the birth centenary of Gandhiji in India. Who is its author?
(a) S. Rangachari   (b) B.R. Nanda
(c) K.G. Saiydan   (d) D.G. Tendulkar

68. Identify the author of *Mahatma Gandhi and Jawaharlal Nehru: A Historical Partnership 1916-1948*.
(a) M.V. Kamath   (b) Madhu Limaye
(c) R.P. Mishra   (d) K. Santhanam

69. Identify the author of *Sarvodaya Order*.
(a) Vishwanath Tandon   (b) Manubehn Gandhi
(c) K.G. Mashruwala   (d) Vinoba Bhave

70. In which year did Gandhiji assume the responsibility for conducting *Indian Opinion*, a weekly?

(a) 1902   (b) 1904
(c) 1906   (d) 1908

71. Besides English, in which Indian language was *Indian Opinion* published in the beginning?
   (a) Tamil   (b) Hindi
   (c) Gujarati   (d) In all the three

72. Identify the author of *Gandhi on World Affairs*.
   (a) Paul F. Power   (b) Romesh Thapar
   (c) Philip Neol-Baker   (d) R.R. Diwakar

73. Who wrote *Gandhiji: A Study* ?
   (a) Pyarelal   (b) Hiren Mukherjee
   (c) G. Ramachandran   (d) K. Santhanam

74. Which of the following works on Gandhiji is the product of B.R. Ambedkar
   (a) *Ranade, Gandhi and Jinnah*
   (b) *What Congress and Gandhi have done to the Untouchables*
   (c) *Searchlight on Gandhi*
   (d) Both (a) and (b)

75. When did Gandhiji publish his epoch-making commentary on *Gita*, of which about 5000 copies were sold within a week of its publication?
   (a) 1915   (b) 1917
   (c) 1919   (d) 1921

76. *Truth and Non-Violence* is the report of the UNESCO symposium on 'Truth and Non-violence in Gandhi's Humanism' organised by UNESCO in collaboration with the Indian National Commission for Co-operation on the occasion of Mahatma Gandhi's

Centennial Celebration in Paris, 14-17 October 1969. It was edited and introduced by
- (a) N.G. Ranga
- (b) T.K. Mahadevan
- (c) S. Chakravarti
- (d) G. Ramachandran

77. *The Volcano*, a novel on the Gandhian revolution, has been written by
- (a) G. Ramachandran
- (b) H.M. Vyas
- (c) A.G. Sheorey
- (d) Sugata Dasgupta

78. Gandhi's *Discourses on the Gita* was translated into English from the original Gujarati by
- (a) V.B. Kher
- (b) V.G. Desai
- (c) Mahadev Desai
- (d) Sushila Nayar

79. Identify the author of *The Murder of Mahatma Gandhi*.
- (a) J.C. Jain
- (b) B.G. Ray
- (c) M.S. Patel
- (d) S.K. Dhawan

80. The Indian Council for Cultural relations brought out a special issue of its English language quarterly, *Indian Horizons*, dedicated to the 125th birth anniversary of Mahatma Gandhi, titled *Gandhi 125 Years*. Who is its editor?
- (a) Rajmohan Gandhi
- (b) S.S. Mukherjee
- (c) B.R. Nanda
- (d) Arun Gandhi

81. Which of the following is the work of N.K. Bose?
- (a) *My Days with Gandhi*
- (b) *Gandhi in Indian Politics*
- (c) Both (a) and (b)
- (d) *The Philosophy of Mahatma Gandhi*

7

Associations and Institutions

1. On which day of May, 1915 was the Satyagraha Ashram founded by Gandhiji at Ahmedabad?
   - (a) 25th
   - (b) 20th
   - (c) 15th
   - (d) 10th

2. Of the various places suggested to Gandhiji for establishing an *ashram* to continue his "experiments" with a life of truth and non-violence, he ultimately chose the city of Ahmedabad. What was the reason for this preference?
   - (a) Being a Gujarati, he thought he could influence the people most through the Gujarati language
   - (b) Since Ahmedabad was an ancient centre of handloom weaving, it was likely to be the most favourable field for the revival of cottage industry.
   - (c) Being the richest trading centre in Gujarat, monetary help from its wealthy citizens would be more available here than elsewhere.
   - (d) All of the above.

3. Who was the principal man to help Gandhiji in getting accommodation for his Satyagraha Ashram?

(a) Shankarlal Banker   (b) Jivanlal Desai
(c) Ambalal Sarabhai   (d) Vallabhbhai Patel

4. With about how many inmates was the Satyagraha Ashram founded?
   (a) Fifteen   (b) Twenty
   (c) Twenty-five   (d) Thirty

5. The admission of an untouchable family into the Satyagraha Ashram (later known as Sabarmati Ashram after the name of the river at Ahmedabad) created a flutter amongst the sympathisers as also led to serious internal frictions. Gandhiji found himself on trial. But ultimately he succeeded in meeting the challenge. Who had referred this family to Gandhiji for admission into the Ashram?
   (a) G.K. Gokhale   (b) Kaka Kalelkar
   (c) N.C. Kelkar   (d) Amritlal Thakkar

6. Gandhiji worked out certain principles and rules of conduct which were to be observed by every inmate of the Satyagraha Ashram. These came to be known as 'vows' for the *Ashramites* to follow. How many such vows were laid out?
   (a) Eleven   (b) Nine
   (c) Seven   (d) Five

7. Soon after its establishment, the Satyagraha Ashram ran out of funds. One day a stranger came and gave to Gandhiji a sum of Rs 13,000. He left without even telling his name. Who was this anonymous donor?
   (a) Ambalal Sarabhai   (b) Jagatbhai
   (c) Shankarlal Parikh   (d) None of them

8. One category of the members of the Satyagraha Ashram was that of students. Both boys and girls, above the age of four years, were admitted as students. They were required to remain in the Ashram for the whole course of studies. The full course of education was planned to last
   (a) Four years   (b) Six years
   (c) Eight years   (d) Ten years

9. When did Gandhiji disband the Satyagraha or Sabarmati Ashram which then became the centre for removal of untouchability?
   (a) 1934   (b) 1933
   (c) 1932   (d) 1931

10. Under its constitution, the All-India Village Industries Association was to work under the guidance and advice of Gandhiji. When was it formed?
    (a) 1930   (b) 1932
    (c) 1934   (d) 1936

11. Where was the All-India Village Industries Association set up?
    (a) Patna   (b) Ahmedabad
    (c) Surat   (d) Wardha

12. Who among the following provided ample land with buildings for the use of the All-India Village Industries Association?
    (a) Jamnalal Bajaj   (b) Shankarlal Banker
    (c) J.C. Kumarappa   (d) Amritlal Thakkar

13. The first All-India Village Industries Exhibition was opened by Gandhiji in April, 1935 at

(a) Ahmedabad   (b) Indore
(c) Nagpur   (d) Delhi

14. Gandhiji founded the All-India Spinners Association in September
    (a) 1925   (b) 1927
    (c) 1931   (d) 1933

15. Every member of the All-India Spinners' Association was under an obligation to
    (a) Propagate *Charkha*
    (b) Wear *Khaddar*
    (c) Spin 1000 yards of yarn per month
    (d) All of the above

16. Identify the incorrect statement in respect of the All-India Spinners Association.
    (a) It was established as an integral part of the Congress organisation.
    (b) It consisted of members, associates and donors with an executive council
    (c) It was set up as an expert organisation for the development of hand-spinning and *Khaddar* with independent existence and powers.
    (d) None of the above

17. Identify the location of Gandhi Shikshan Bhawan.
    (a) Allahabad   (b) Varanasi
    (c) Bombay   (d) Bhopal

18. When did Gandhiji settle down at the Sevagram Ashram?
    (a) 1934   (b) 1936
    (c) 1938   (d) 1939

19. When was Gandhiji's Wardha Ashram established?
    (a) 1927   (b) 1929
    (c) 1931   (d) 1933

20. Gandhi Seva Sangh, established in 1923, conducts research work and assessment of the Gandhian thought and constructive programme for the establishment of a non-violent society. Where is it located?
    (a) Bombay   (b) Wardha
    (c) Ahmedabad   (d) Pune

21. Immediately after his epic fast in Yeravda Prison, Gandhiji founded the Harijan Sevak Sangh for the removal of untouchability through truth and non-violence. The Sangh came into existence in 1932 in the month of
    (a) July   (b) August
    (c) September   (d) November

22. Where is the Central Office of the Harijan Sevak Sangh?
    (a) Delhi   (b) Patna
    (c) Wardha   (d) Nagpur

23. The Harijan Sevak Sangh, founded by Gandhiji, was first known as the
    (a) Society for Abolition of Untouchability
    (b) Anti-Untouchability League
    (c) Servants of Untouchable Society
    (d) None of the above

24. The Gandhi Ashram at Varanasi was established as early as 1922 by a group of persons who left Banaras

Hindu University on the call given by Gandhiji. Who was its first Director?

(a) Lal Bahadur Shastri

(b) Purushottam Das Tandon

(c) Rajendra Prasad

(d) J.B. Kripalani

25. The opening ceremony of which of the following was performed by Gandhiji at Wardha on December 30, 1938?

(a) Magan Museum   (b) Udyog Bhawan

(c) Charkha Sangh   (d) Both (a) and (b)

26. Identify the year in which Birla House, New Delhi, where Gandhiji very often used to stay and where he was shot dead, was turned into a government-run Gandhi museum.

(a) 1956   (b) 1965

(c) 1971   (d) 1974

27. Gandhigram was founded in 1947 at

(a) Wardha   (b) Madurai

(c) Ahmedabad   (d) Madras

28. Who founded the Gandhigram?

(a) Vinoba Bhave   (b) G. Ramachandran

(c) T.S. Soundaram   (d) Both (b) and (c)

29. Who founded the Gandhi Hindustani Sahitya Sabha?

(a) Gopinath Bordoloi (b) Kaka Kalelkar

(c) G.B. Pant   (d) Rajendra Prasad

30. Where is the Gandhi Hindustani Sahitya Sabha located?

(a) Madras   (b) Guwahati
(c) New Delhi   (d) Agra

31. When was the Gandhi Peace Foundation established?
    (a) 1960   (b) 1958
    (c) 1956   (d) 1954

32. Gandhi Peace Foundation is located at
    (a) New Delhi   (b) Bombay
    (c) Wardha   (d) Calcutta

33. Who was the first Chairman of the Gandhi Peace Foundation?
    (a) U.N. Dhebar   (b) R.R. Diwakar
    (c) Indira Gandhi   (d) Morarji Desai

34. The Gandhi Peace Foundation organised an International Peace Conference in New Delhi in 1962 to plead for the cessation of the manufacture, testing and stockpiling of nuclear armaments. About how many delegates, representing the leading peace movements of the world, attended it?
    (a) 80   (b) 100
    (c) 120   (d) 130

35. The Gandhi Peace Foundation runs four Schools of Non-Violence. Three of them are in New Delhi, Madras and Madurai. Where is the fourth?
    (a) Calicut   (b) Ranchi
    (c) Allahabad   (d) Ahmedabad

36. Identify the founder of the Gandhian Institute of Studies.

(a) Jawaharlal Nehru   (b) Morarji Desai
(c) G.B. Pant   (d) Jayprakash Narayan

37. Navjeevan Prakashan Mandir was established by Gandhiji in
   (a) 1915   (b) 1917
   (c) 1919   (d) 1921

38. Navjeevan Prakashan Mandir is engaged in the publication of literature for the propagation of Gandhian thought. Where is it located?
   (a) Wardha   (b) Ahmedabad
   (c) New Delhi   (d) Bombay

39. How many Gandhi Museums have been set up throughout the country by the Gandhi Memorial Trust?
   (a) Nine   (b) Seven
   (c) Five   (d) Four

40. At which Gandhi Museum is the blood-stained *dhoti*, which Gandhiji was wearing when he was shot dead, preserved?
   (a) Madurai Museum   (b) Delhi Museum
   (c) Patna Museum   (d) Bombay Museum

41. Gandhiji's last surviving pair of spectacles is still preserved in the Gandhi Museum at
   (a) Delhi   (b) Patna
   (c) Madurai   (d) Barrackpore

42. How many personal articles of Gandhiji are displayed at the Madurai Museum?
   (a) Fourteen   (b) Ten
   (c) Eight   (d) Six

43. The photostat copies of how many letters, written by Gandhiji, are available in the library attached to the Madurai Gandhi Museum?
    (a) 15,000   (b) 18,000
    (c) 22,000   (d) 27,000

44. A special attraction of one of the Gandhi Museum is the exhibition depicting Gandhiji's life through figurines prepared by Sushila Patel. Identify the place of this museum.
    (a) Patna   (b) Bombay
    (c) Delhi   (d) Madurai

45. The objective of the Maganwadi Sangrahalaya Samiti is the collection and exhibition of models and samples of *Khadi* and village industries products. Gandhiji established it in 1938 at
    (a) Ahmedabad   (b) Bhopal
    (c) Wardha   (d) Sholapur

46. The Gandhi Smriti and Darshan Samiti, Tees January Marg, New Delhi, tries to promote Gandhian ideals through various programmes. When was it established?
    (a) 1975   (b) 1980
    (c) 1984   (d) 1988

47. Who is the ex-officio Chairman of the Gandhi Smriti and Darshan Samiti, New Delhi?
    (a) Vice-President of India
    (b) Prime Minister of India
    (c) Lt. Governor of Delhi
    (d) Chief Minister of Delhi

48. The basic objective of Gandhi Ghars is to serve as centres for the all-round uplift of villages. Though the idea of building a number of Gandhi Ghars was advocated by Jawaharlal Nehru as early as 1949, the scheme acquired concrete shape only in
(a) 1953   (b) 1955
(c) 1957   (d) 1960

49. Which state in the country has the largest number of Gandhi Ghars?
(a) Karnataka   (b) Gujarat
(c) Uttar Pradesh   (d) Kerala

50. For the production of films on the life and thought of Gandhiji and people's education through their exhibition, the Gandhi Films Committee was set up in
(a) 1950   (b) 1952
(c) 1954   (d) 1955

51. At which place was the Gandhi Films Committee set up?
(a) Madras   (b) Pune
(c) Bombay   (d) New Delhi

52. The first film completed by the Gandhi Films Committee was the 'Voice of India', a film of an hour's duration. This film was completed in
(a) 1953   (b) 1955
(c) 1956   (d) 1957

53. An agreement for the production of films was reached between the Gandhi Films Committee and the Films Division of the Government of India which came into effect from 1958. When was the film titled *Mahatma* completed and released?

(a) 1966   (b) 1968
(c) 1970   (d) 1972

54. Which of the following short documentary on Gandhiji has been produced by the Gandhi Smarak Nidhi?
    (a) *Harijan*
    (b) *The last Journey*
    (c) *His Memory We Cherish*
    (d) All of the three

55. The production of Gandhi films has been a major preoccupation of the Gandhi Smarak Nidhi. The earliest film material available with the Nidhi dates back to
    (a) 1912   (b) 1920
    (c) 1922   (d) 1929

56. The Gandhi Smarak Nidhi (Central) i.e. the Gandhi National Memorial Trust has been set up to act as an information centre of the Gandhian work as also to foster ideological study among the workers. Identify its place of location.
    (a) Bombay   (b) New Delhi
    (c) Ahmedabad   (d) Wardha

57. Around how many million people, rich and poor, contributed to the fund of the Gandhi Memorial Trust as a homage to the memory of the Father of the Nation?
    (a) Eight   (b) Ten
    (c) Twelve   (d) Fifteen

58. Identify the State which made the largest contribution to the Gandhi Memorial Fund?

(a) Maharashtra   (b) Uttar Pradesh
(c) Gujarat   (d) Bengal

59. Where are the headquarters of the Uttar Pradesh Gandhi Smarak Nidhi?
    (a) Allahabad   (b) Lucknow
    (c) Sevapuri   (d) Agra

60. The Delhi Gandhi Smarak Nidhi came into existence in 1956. Who was its first Chairman?
    (a) Gopinath Aman
    (b) Sucheta Kripalani
    (c) Brij Kishore Chandiwala
    (d) Yudhvir Singh

61. Which of the following statements in respect of the Gandhi Hill at Vijaywada is incorrect?
    (a) The Gandhi Stupa has been created in accordance with the plan of Nandlal Bose
    (b) The corner-stone for children's park and sound and light was laid by V.V. Giri
    (c) Besides the Gandhi Stupa, the Gandhi Hill has a Library Hall and a Conference Hall.
    (d) None of the above

62. Identify the year in which Gandhiji founded the Passive Resistance Association in South Africa where at every meeting the political situation was explained and oaths of resistance were administered afresh.
    (a) 1908   (b) 1907
    (c) 1906   (d) 1905

63. Gandhi Bhawans have been conceived of as centres of manifold academic studies in Gandhian and allied thought as also for social service programmes

suiting the students. The foundation stone of the first Gandhi Bhawan was laid by Jawaharlal Nehru in December 1959 at
(a) Wardha
(b) Bombay
(c) Allahabad
(d) Delhi

64. Mahatma Gandhi University was established in 1983 at
(a) Kottayam
(b) Hyderabad
(c) Madurai
(d) Cuttack

65. The Gandhi Institute for Non-Violence was established in 1991 in
(a) U.K.
(b) U.S.A
(c) France
(d) Canada

66. Who established the Gandhi Institute, for Non-Violence?
(a) Arun Gandhi
(b) B.R. Nanda
(c) Nelson Mandela
(d) None of the above

67. The Aga Khan Palace Gandhi National Memorial, Pune, has been set up to maintain the Palace as a National Memorial Museum with a picture gallery and to carry on women's welfare activities. When was it established?
(a) 1968
(b) 1970
(c) 1972
(d) 1974

68. Kasturba Gandhi National Memorial Trust is engaged in the task of integrated uplift of women and children in rural areas. Where is it located?
(a) Wardha
(b) Indore
(c) Surat
(d) Rajkot

69. The anti-leprosy work was very dear to Gandhiji. To promote this work in a systematic manner, the Gandhi Memorial Leprosy Foundation was established, after the death of Gandhiji, in
    (a) 1949   (b) 1951
    (c) 1953   (d) 1955

70. Where are the headquarters of the Gandhi Memorial Leprosy Foundation?
    (a) New Delhi   (b) Pune
    (c) Kottayam   (d) Wardha

71. Gandhi Information Centre is a charitable membership organisation. It serves as a research and education centre for non-violence. Its main objectives are to promote the work of Gandhiji as well as the ethics of non-violence in the western world. Where is it based?
    (a) Berlin   (b) Paris
    (c) New York   (d) London

72. The 1994 International Gandhi Award of the Mahatma Gandhi Leprosy Foundation was presented by the President of India to
    (a) V. Ekambaran   (b) Joon Lew
    (c) G.B. Oka   (d) Both (a) and (b)

73. Father Dominique Pire founded the Mahatma Gandhi University of Peace in
    (a) U.S.A.   (b) Belgium
    (c) Canada   (d) France

74. Jamnalal Bajaj Awards are given for distinguished services to society and propagating Gandhian ideals.

Each award carries a citation, a trophy and cash prize of
(a) Rs 1 lakh   (b) Rs. 1.5 lakh
(c) Rs 2 lakh   (d) Rs 2.5 lakh

75. How many eminent person were chosen for the 1994 Jamnalal Bajaj Awards for the promotion of Gandhian values and ideals?
(a) Six   (b) Four
(c) Three   (d) Two

76. Which Gandhian institution brings out the monthly magazine *Sansthakul*?
(a) Gandhi Smarak Nidhi
(b) Gandhi Peace Foundation
(c) Gandhi Vichar Parishad
(d) Gandhi Hindustan Sahitya Sabha

77. Through the efforts of eminent Gandhians like Kakasaheb Kalelkar, Shankara Deo and K.G. Mashruwala the Gandhi Vichar Parishad, with its headquarters at Wardha, was formed in 1951 to promote research work and study of Gandhian thought. When was it merged in the Gandhi Smarak Nidhi?
(a) 1955   (b) 1959
(c) 1961   (d) 1965

78. The Mahatma Gandhi Human Rights Organisation of Budapest seeks to improve the social status of ethnic groups, especially Asian, African and Jewish in Hungary. When was it formed?
(a) 1988   (b) 1990
(c) 1992   (d) 1994

79. The International Gandhi Award, instituted by the Mahatma Gandhi Leprosy Foundation, represents an acknowledgement of the contribution of those who have dedicated their lives to the cause of the struggle against leprosy. Besides a citation, the Award carries a sum of
(a) Rs 2.5 lakh   (b) Rs 2 lakh
(c) Rs 1.5 lakh   (d) Rs 1 lakh

80. The International Gandhian Movement and its sister body, Campaign Against Violence, have started taking roots in
(a) Australia   (b) Canada
(c) Belgium   (d) France

81. When was the International Gandhian Movement founded?
(a) 1994   (b) 1991
(c) 1990   (d) 1988

82. The objective of the Trusteeship Club, established in 1975, is to spread the ideal of trusteeship as propounded by Mahatma Gandhi as also to provide training to people to take up work in this direction. Identify the place of its location.
(a) Madras   (b) Madurai
(c) Hyderabad   (d) Calcutta

83. Sriniketan at Madras is engaged in spreading the message of Gandhiji through meetings, exhibition of books, night classes, cultural camps, etc. It is the only institution in the country where all the Indian languages are taught through the Nagri script as advocated by Gandhiji. When was it established?

(a) 1963   (b) 1965
(c) 1967   (d) 1969

84. Gandhiji laid great stress on the promotion of *Khadi* for the country's freedom and economic development. After the attainment of Independence, the Government passed the All-India Khadi and Village Industries Commission Act, thus institutionalising the process of *Khadi's* promotion. When was this Act promulgated?
    (a) 1961   (b) 1956
    (c) 1953   (d) 1951

85. Through "Ashram Gandhi", Gedong B. Oka is making a valiant effort to carry on the traditions of spirituality and creating awareness about Gandhiji's thoughts and his way of *ashram* life. In which Island of Indonesia is Ashram Gandhi located?
    (a) Java   (b) Bali
    (c) Sumatra   (d) Borneo

8

Contemporaries

1. Identify Gandhiji's contemporary who made this observation about him: "He laughs like a child and adores children".
   - (a) C.F. Andrews
   - (b) W.W. Pearson
   - (c) Rabindranath Tagore
   - (d) B.G. Tilak

2. Who did Gandhiji hail as his "political *guru*"?
   - (a) Dadabhai Naoroji
   - (b) M.G. Ranade
   - (c) G.K. Gokhale
   - (d) Pherozeshah Mehta

3. Khan Abdul Ghaffar Khan joined Gandhiji in the struggle initiated by him for the country's freedom and in this connection he was imprisoned several times. About how many years of his life did he spend in prison?
   - (a) Sixteen
   - (b) Fourteen
   - (c) Eleven
   - (d) Nine

4. Who called Gandhiji as the "permanent super President of the Congress"?
   - (a) Jawaharlal Nehru
   - (b) Sarojini Naidu
   - (c) Vallabhbhai Patel
   - (d) M.A. Jinnah

5. When did Mahadev Desai join Gandhiji as his Secretary?
   (a) July, 1917   (b) November, 1917
   (c) August, 1916   (d) December, 1916

6. For about how long Mahadev Desai served Gandhiji as his secretary?
   (a) 15 years   (b) 20 years
   (c) 25 years   (d) 30 years

7. Who described Gandhiji "as a good little man"?
   (a) Winston Churchil   (b) Lord Irwin
   (c) Stafford Cripps   (d) Lord Halifax

8. Identify the Gandhian leader, who came to be described as the 'Bhism Pitamah' of Indian politics.
   (a) Vallabhbhai Patel
   (b) Morarji Desai
   (c) Kamaraj
   (d) Madan Mohan Malaviya

9. One of the eminent Gandhians gave the slogan 'Jai Jagat'. Who was he?
   (a) Lal Bahadur Shastri (b) Rajendra Prasad
   (c) Vinoba Bhave   (d) Kaka Kalelkar

10. Who was described by Gandhiji as a "Prince of Patriots"?
    (a) Subhas Chandra Bose (b) Vallabhbhai Patel
    (c) Jawaharlal Nehru   (d) B.G. Tilak

11. Inspired by Gandhiji, Gopinath Bordoloi gave up his legal practice and joined the national movement in
    (a) 1931   (b) 1929
    (c) 1924   (d) 1921

12. A veteran freedom fighter and a true Gandhian, Gopinath Bordoloi was instrumental in the establishment of
    (a) Kamrup Akademy
    (b) B. Boroah College
    (c) Assam Medical College
    (d) All of the three

13. One of the exceptionally bright star of Gandhian galaxy, Morarji Desai had the rare honour of receiving the highest national awards of both India and Pakistan, namely Bharat Ratna and Nishan-i-Pakistan. How old was he when he received the Pakistan award?
    (a) 96   (b) 92
    (c) 88   (d) 85

14. Mahatma Gandhi remained the Chancellor of the Gujarat Vidyapeeth for 19 years from 1929 to 1948. For about how many years had Morarji Desai been the Chancellor of the Vidyapeeth?
    (a) 25   (b) 29
    (c) 33   (d) 36

15. Identify the Indian socialist who made a rapid transition from a rebel to a devotee of Gandhiji, and spent the rest of his life in the post-Quit India period in expounding and invoking Gandhian concepts and method.
    (a) Narendra Dev
    (b) Jayaprakash Narayan
    (c) Yusuf Meherally
    (d) M.N. Roy

16. Greatly inspired by Gandhiji's ideas, a well-known personality of the world observed: "Jesus Christ gave the motivation and Gandhi showed the method. Gandhi was probably the first person in history to lift the love ethic of Jesus above mere interaction between individuals to a powerful and effective social force on a large scale". Identify the personality.
    (a) Martin Luther King (b) Nelson Mandela
    (c) Albert Einstein (d) Aldous Huxley

17. Identify the place where Gandhiji for the first time came in close contact with Motilal Nehru in 1919.
    (a) Delhi (b) Lahore
    (c) Allahabad (d) Amritsar

18. Who first hailed Gandhiji as 'Mahatma' when he returned to the country after his successful struggle in South Africa?
    (a) G.K. Gokhale
    (b) Lajpat Rai
    (c) C.R. Das
    (d) Rabindranath Tagore

19. G. Ramachandran played a leading role in spreading the teachings of Gandhiji for several decades. When did he join Sabarmati Ashram?
    (a) 1920 (b) 1922
    (c) 1924 (d) 1926

20. Who among the following received the Mahatma Gandhi Peace Award for the year 1994, instituted by the National Federation of Indian American Association?

(a) B.R. Nanda   (b) Morarji Desai
(c) Rajmohan Gandhi   (d) Vasant Sathe

21. Identify the ardent admirer and close associate of Gandhiji who was fondly called "Mamaji".
    (a) Kaka Kalelkar
    (b) Jamnalal Bajaj
    (c) G. Ramachandran
    (d) Kishorlal Ghai Mashruwala

22. Which of the following parallel in the lives of Gandhiji and Martin Luther King is not correct?
    (a) Both led large political movements using the method of *satyagraha*.
    (b) Both were votaries of non-violence.
    (c) Both were lawyers.
    (d) Both died by the bullet.

23. Who of the following associates of Gandhiji was an advocate by profession before joining the national movement?
    (a) Rajendra Prasad   (b) Motilal Nehru
    (c) Vallabhbhai Patel   (d) All of them

24. A close associate and co-worker, Vallabhbhai Patel participated in all the movements launched under the leadership of Gandhiji. In recognition of his great success in organising the *Satyagraha* Movement at a particular place, Gandhiji gave him the title of '*Sardar*'. Which was that place?
    (a) Kheda   (b) Bardoli
    (c) Ahmedabad   (d) Champaran

25. Inspired by Gandhiji's appeal, Subhas Chandra Bose resigned from the Indian Civil Service and joined the national movement at the age of
    (a) 32   (b) 30
    (c) 28   (d) 25

26. Subhas Chandra Bose defeated Gandhiji's official candidate for the Presidentship of the Indian National Congress at the historic Tripuri session of the Congress in March 1939. Identify Gandhiji's nominee.
    (a) Rajendra Prasad
    (b) Maulana Abul Kalam Azad
    (c) Pattabhi Sitaramayya
    (d) Vallabhbhai Patel

27. The differences with Gandhiji led Subhas Chandra Bose to resign the Presidentship of the India National Congress in 1939. Leaving the Congress, he formed a new party called
    (a) Swatantra Party   (b) Forward Bloc
    (c) Praja Socialist Party (d) None of the above

28. Addressing to Gandhiji, one of his associates uttered these words: "I am going soon, Mahatmaji, and I shall not be here to see *swaraj*. But I know that you have won it and will soon have it". Who was he?
    (a) Lajpat Rai   (b) C.R. Das
    (c) Motilal Nehru   (d) Ajmal Khan

29. Who described Gandhiji as "the greatest Indian since Gautama Buddha and the greatest man since Jesus Christ"?
    (a) Nelson Mandela   (b) Horace Alexander
    (c) J.H. Holmes   (d) Kenneth K. Kaunda

30. How old was G.D. Birla when he first met Gandhiji in 1915?
    (a) Nineteen   (b) Twenty-one
    (c) Twenty-three   (d) Twenty-five

31. The correspondence between Gandhiji and G.D. Birla began in
    (a) 1924   (b) 1926
    (c) 1928   (d) 1930

32. Vinoba Bhave is generally regarded as the nearest and truest follower of Gandhiji. When he first met Gandhiji?
    (a) 1916   (b) 1918
    (c) 1919   (d) 1920

33. Who was entrusted with the task of writing Gandhiji's daily diary after the death of Mahadev Desai?
    (a) Sushila Nayar   (b) Mirabehn
    (c) J.B. Kripalani   (d) Abha Gandhi

34. Who was, according to Gandhiji, the real founder of the Indian nationalist movement?
    (a) M.G. Ranade   (b) Dadabhai Naoroji
    (c) B.G. Tilak   (d) Ram Mohan Roy

35. Identify the person who gave Gandhiji his first real lesson in *ahimsa* by teaching him to apply heroic passivity to public life by fighting evil not by evil, but by love.
    (a) Ganesh Vasudev Joshi
    (b) Narayan Chandavarkar
    (c) Dadabhai Naoroji
    (d) Rajchandra

36. Who described the jails in the country as "Mahatma Gandhi University?"
    (a) Madhu Limaye
    (b) Jawaharlal Nehru
    (c) Sarojini Naidu
    (d) Maulana Abul Kalam Azad

37. Identify the associate who pressed Gandhiji to move to Wardha in September 1933.
    (a) J.B. Kripalani   (b) Jamnalal Bajaj
    (c) Kaka Kalelkar   (d) N.B. Khare

38. Much inspired by Gandhian ideas a well-known reformer and fighter for social rights observed: "There is no choice between violence and non-violence. The only choice we have is between non-violence and perishing." Identify him
    (a) Martin Luther King   (b) Nelson Mandela
    (c) G. Ramachandaran   (d) Vinoba Bhave

39. On his arrival in Bombay in 1915 after his successful struggle in South Africa, Gandhiji stayed for a few days at Santa Cruz in the house of
    (a) Pherozeshah Mehta   (b) B.G. Horniman
    (c) Revashankar Jhaveri (d) Narottam Morarji

40. One of the most spectacular embodiment of the Gandhian legacy of *satyagraha* in the post-Gandhian era is to be found in the work and person of Martin Luther King. When was he awarded the Noble Peace Prize?
    (a) 1968   (b) 1964
    (c) 1962   (d) 1960

41. The "Practical Trusteeship Formula" was drawn up by two close associates of Gandhiji which, with a few changes, received Gandhiji's approval. One of them was Kishorlal Mashruwala. Who was the other?
   (a) Narhari Parikh   (b) Vinoba Bhave
   (c) J.B. Kripalani   (d) A.V. Thakkar

42. Who of the following co-workers of Gandhiji was awarded Bharat Ratna by the Government after Independence?
   (a) Khan Abdul Gaffar Khan
   (b) Purushottam Das Tandon
   (c) Both (a) and (b)
   (d) Gopinath Bordoloi

43. Identify the well-known personality of Gandhiji's time who paid this tribute to him: "Gandhiji's epithet (Mahatma) is not just honorific. He was indeed 'a great soul'. He may have been the greatest of any that have made their appearance in our time. He was undoubtedly the peer of the greatest souls of previous ages from which we have surviving records of outstanding personalities"
   (a) Arnold Joseph Toynbee
   (b) Louis Fischer
   (c) S. Radhakrishnan
   (d) Jawaharlal Nehru

44. A close associate of Mahatma Gandhi and a veteran freedom fighter, Abha Gandhi joined the freedom struggle at the age of
   (a) Twenty-eight   (b) Twenty-five
   (c) Twenty-one   (d) Fifteen

45. Who of the following Englishmen made this observation about Gandhiji? "In my judgement, Gandhi was a great a benefactor of my country as he was of his own. Gandhi made it impossible for the British to go on ruling India, but at the same time he made it possible for us to abdicate without rancour and without dishonour."
    (a) Harold Wilson
    (b) Arnold Joseph Toynbee
    (c) Lord Attenborough
    (d) Lord Listowel

46. Identify the Viceroy who wrote home these words after his first meeting with Gandhiji:
    "Mr Gandhi's religious and moral views are, I believe, admirable, but I confess that I find it diffi-cult to understand the practice of them in politics."
    (a) Lord Irwin   (b) Lord Willingdon
    (c) Lord Reading   (d) None of the above

47. While Gandhiji was on his first visit to Shantiniketan in 1915, he got the sad news of the death of a distinguished leader and politician of the country. Who was he?
    (a) B.G. Tilak
    (b) G.K. Gokhale
    (c) Surendranath Banerjee
    (d) Lajpat Rai

48. Gandhiji chose to use Sudhir Ghosh as his emissary for the negotiation with the British Government during 1945-47. How old was Sudhir Ghosh at that time?

(a) 42 years   (b) 38 years
(c) 33 years   (d) 29 years

49. Identify the freedom fighter who plunged into the Gandhi's 'Quit India' movement in 1942, but after Independence left the Congress and formed the S-ocialist Party of India.
    (a) Madhu Limaye   (b) N.G. Goray
    (c) Achut Patwardhan   (d) Yusuf Meherally

50. Which of the following observations about Gandhiji was made by General Smuts of South Africa?
    (a) "The saint has left our shores. I sincerely hope for ever."
    (b) "It was my fate to be the antagonist of a man for whom even then I had the highest respect."
    (c) "Men like him redeem us all from a sense of commonplaceness and futility and are an inspiration to us not to be weary in well-doing."
    (d) All of the above.

51. Identify the close associate of Gandhiji who offered this tribute to him when he started his historic salt march: "Today the pilgrim marches onward on his long trek; staff in hand he goes along the dusty roads, clear eyed and firm of step with his faithful band trudging along behind him. The fire of a great resolve is in him and surpassing love of his miserable countrymen and love of truth that scorches and love of freedom that inspires."
    (a) C.F. Andrews   (b) Jawaharlal Nehru
    (c) Sarojini Naidu   (d) C.R. Das

52. In the course of a conversation with C.F. Andrews, Gandhiji referred to one of his devoted followers in

the following words: "He is a rare gem. He has come to enrich us with his virtue. He has come not to receive, but to give." Who was he?
(a) Vinoba Bhave   (b) Kaka Kalelkar
(c) Mahadev Desai   (d) Pyarelal

53. Who assessed Gandhiji's plan for the country's freedom in these words?
"My reason told me clearly, again and again, that there was a deplorable lack of clarity in the plan which the Mahatma had formulated and that he himself did not have clear idea of the successive stages of the campaign which would bring India to her cherished goal of freedom".
(a) C.R. Das
(b) Subhas Chandra Bose
(c) B.R. Ambedkar
(d) Annie Besant

54. Identify the contemporary who described Gandhiji's Harijan tour in the following words:
"It would be known in the history of Hindu religion as the greatest single effort for reawakening the conscience of Hindu society and for service of the Harijans."
(a) Vinoba Bhave
(b) Madan Mohan Malaviya
(c) G.D. Birla
(d) Jagjivan Ram

55. Mridulabehn Ambalal Sarabhai was with Gandhiji in Noakhali during the communal riots and actively worked for the rehabilitation of refugees after

Partition. Which of the following statements about her is not correct?

(a) She came into contact with Gandhiji in 1918 along with her parents.

(b) She courted imprisonment several times during the freedom struggle.

(c) She was adept in organising Banar Sena of boys and girls.

(d) None of the above.

56. With which of the following was Mridulabehn Ambalal Sarabhai, one of the devoted followers of Gandhiji, closely associated

(a) Sarva Seva Sangh   (b) Insane Biradari

(c) Both (a) and (b)   (d) Gujarat Vidyapeeth

57. Identify the Englishman who contemptuously referred to Gandhiji as a "half-naked *faqir*."

(a) Lord Willingdon   (b) Winston Churchill

(c) Ramsay MacDonald   (d) Lord Wavell

58. Who one of the following close associates of Gandhiji came to be affectionately known as '*Deena-bandhu*' i.e. brother of the poor and the afflicted?

(a) C.F. Andrews

(b) Kaka Kalelkar

(c) A.V. Thakkar

(d) Madan Mohan Malaviya

59. Identify the personality who paid this tribute to Gandhiji:

"As he grew older, his body seemed to be just a vehicle for the mighty spirit within him. Almost one forgot the body as one listened to him or looked at

him, and so where he sat became a temple and where he trod was a hallowed ground."
(a) Sarojini Naidu
(b) Jawaharlal Nehru
(c) Maulana Abul Kalam Azad
(d) S. Radhakrishnan

60. Who was probably the first Indian leader to appreciate the greatness of Gandhiji, remarking that he would be the future leader of the country?
(a) Rabindranath Tagore (b) B.G. Tilak
(c) G.K. Gokhale (d) Dadabhai Naoroji

61. Identify the close associate of Gandhiji on whose death he issued the following press statement:
"My position is worse than a widow's. By a faithful life, she can appropriate the merits of her husband. I can appropriate nothing. What I have lost through his death is a loss forever: 'Rock of ages, cleft for me, let me hide myself in thee'."
(a) Lajpat Rai (b) Motilal Nehru
(c) Ajmal Khan (d) C.R. Das

62. At which session the Indian National Congress held in 1909, did Gopal Krishna Gokhale pay this tribute to Gandhiji?
"It is one of the privileges of my life that I know Mr Gandhi intimately and I can tell you that a purer, a nobler, a braver and a more exalted spirit has never moved on this earth".
(a) Lahore (b) Bombay
(c) Lucknow (d) Ahmedabad

63. Who paid this memorable tribute to Gandhiji?

"Generations to come, it may be, will scarce believe that such as this ever in flesh and blood walked upon this earth."
(a) Romain Rolland   (b) Albert Einstein
(c) Rabindranath Tagore (d) Aldous Huxley

64. The devoted disciple and close associate of Gandhiji, Mirabehn was awarded Padma Vibhushan by the Government in
    (a) 1982   (b) 1984
    (c) 1986   (d) 1988

65. Maulana Abul Kalam Azad, one of the eminent national leaders of the country, met Gandhiji for the first time on January 18, 1920 in Delhi. Where was he born?
    (a) Lahore   (b) Mecca
    (c) Peshawar   (d) Aligarh

66. A trusted colleague of Gandhiji, Maulana Abul Kalam Azad had the distinction of being the youngest President of the Indian National Congress when he was elected to that post in 1923. How old was he then?
    (a) 31 years   (b) 33 years
    (c) 35 years   (d) 37 years

67. Maulana Abul Kalam Azad took active part in the country's struggle for freedom launched by Gandhiji. He was imprisoned a number of times. About how many years of his life did he spend in various jails?
    (a) Five years   (b) Seven years
    (c) Nine years   (d) Eleven years

68. Jawaharlal Nehru differed with Gandhiji on a number of issues, yet he remained very close to him. He was younger to Gandhiji by about
    (a) Ten years   (b) Twelve years
    (c) Sixteen years   (d) Twenty years

69. During the freedom movement launched by Gandhiji, Jawaharlal Nehru was arrested and imprisoned a number of times. In all for how many days he remained in jails?
    (a) 2110   (b) 2632
    (c) 2980   (d) 3262

70. At the suggestion of Gandhiji, Jawaharlal Nehru was elected the President of the Congress at its Lahore session where 'Poorna Swarajya' was laid down as the objective of the Congress. Identify the year of this session
    (a) 1931   (b) 1930
    (c) 1929   (d) 1928

71. One of the most eminent leaders, enjoying Gandhiji's support and confidence, Jawaharlal Nehru became the first Prime Minister of India after independence. For about how many years did he serve the country as Prime Minister?
    (a) Seventeen   (b) Fifteen
    (c) Fourteen   (d) Twelve

72. Identify the leader who last met Gandhiji for about an hour and left him just few minutes before he was shot dead on January 30, 1948 while on his way to the prayer meeting.
    (a) Vallabhbhai Patel
    (b) Rajendra Prasad

(c) Maulana Abul Kalam Azad

(d) Jawaharlal Nehru

73. Who of the following associates of Gandhiji was often called the 'Iron Man of India'?
(a) Madan Mohan Malaviya
(b) Vallabhbhai Patel
(c) Jawaharlal Nehru
(d) Lajpat Rai

74. How many times was Vijay Lakshmi Pandit, sister of Jawaharlal Nehru and a prominent national leader, imprisoned in connection with the Civil Disobedience Movement led by Gandhiji?
(a) Once   (b) Twice
(c) Thrice   (d) Four times

75. One of the foreign friends of Gandhiji observed that "he was a mystic, but he was a very matter-of-fact mystic: no dreamer of heavenly dreams, no visionary, who saw things unutterable when in a state trance. When the inner voice spoke to Gandhi, it was only to tell him what to do tomorrow — how to act more effectively to bring union of hearts between Hindus and Muslims or how to hasten the downfall of untouchability." Identify him.
(a) Horace Alexander   (b) C.F. Andrews
(c) Louis Fischer   (d) Dennis Dalton

76. Rajchandra (or Rajchandbhai as Gandhiji called him) came nearest to being Gandhiji's religious 'Guru' or mentor. How many years older was he than Gandhiji?
(a) Fifteen   (b) Ten
(c) Seven   (d) Two

77. On his very first meeting with a person, Gandhiji was convinced that he was a man of great character and learning. He was also known as a *Shatavadhani*, i.e. one having the faculty of remembering or attending to a hundred things simultaneously. Who was he?
    (a) Revashankar Jagjivan
    (b) Rajchandra
    (c) Chandavarkar
    (d) G.S. Iyer

78. Identify the three 'moderns' who left a deep impress on Gandhiji's life and captivated him by their living or writings.
    (a) Gokhale, Tilak and Tagore
    (b) Ranade, Tagore and Ruskin
    (c) Tolstoy, Ruskin and Rajchandra
    (d) Ruskin, Tagore and Gokhale

79. Who of the following associates of Gandhiji was the founder of Bhartiya Vidya Bhavan?
    (a) K.M. Munshi
    (b) Jamnalal Bajaj
    (c) Madan Mohan Malaviya
    (d) Govind Ballabh Pant

80. A disciple of Gandhiji whom he first met on English soil in July 1914, V.V. Giri after Independence served as the Governor of
    (a) Uttar Pradesh   (b) Kerala
    (c) Mysore   (d) All the three

81. Like Gandhiji, B.R. Ambedkar worked with all sincerity and devotion for the eradication of the evil practice of untouchability in the Hindu society. He

resorted to *satyagraha* for getting Hindu temples thrown open to untouchables. With which of the following is his name associated?

(a) Parvati *Satyagraha* in Pune
(b) Kalaram *Satyagraha* in Nasik
(c) Ambabai *Satyagraha* in Amravati
(d) All the above

82. Who of the following contemporaries of Gandhiji played a leading role in getting provision of special significance for the Scheduled Castes and Scheduled Tribes incorporated in the Constitution of India?

(a) A.V. Thakkar   (b) B.R. Ambedkar
(c) M.R. Jayakar   (d) Both (a) and (b)

83. One of the following associates founded the Samaj Samata Sangh to propagate the gospel of social equality among untouchables and upper caste Hindus, a cause so dear to Gandhiji. Who was he?

(a) Jagjivan Ram   (b) B.R. Ambedkar
(c) M.C. Rajah   (d) A.V. Thakkar

84. Who of the following was called by Gandhiji not as a prospective *ashramite,* but primarily to teach in the Ashram National School?

(a) Kaka Kalelkar
(b) Kishorlal Mashruwala
(c) Both (a) and (b)
(d) Vinoba Bhave

85. Identify the eminent personality who made the following memorable statement on the night of the day of Gandhiji's murder.

"The light has gone out of our lives and there is darkness everywhere..... The light has gone out, I said, and yet I was wrong. For the light that shone in this country was no ordinary light. The light that has illumined this country for these many many years will illumine this country for many more years, and a thousand years later that light will be seen in this count. y and the world will see it, and it will give solace to our innumerable hearts."

(a) Sarojini Naidu
(b) Jawaharlal Nehru
(c) S. Radhakrishnan
(d) Maulana Abul Kalam Azad

9

Photo Quiz

1. Gandhiji regarded him as his political "*guru*". Who is he?

2. At the call of Gandhiji, he gave up his flourishing legal practice and joined the national movement. He also gifted his palace to the national cause. Identify him.

3. A follower and a close associate of Gandhiji, she took a leading part in the country's freedom struggle and was a gifted scholar of the English language. Who is she?

4. Identify this eminent Gandhian who actively participated in all the political movements launched by Gandhiji and suffered imprisonment for quite many years. He came to be popularly known as Frontier Gandhi.

5. Gandhiji is seen here exchanging notes with two great leaders of the country. One is Jawaharlal Nehru. Who is the other?

6. Identify the location of this famous hut of Gandhiji.

7. Gandhiji at the bedside of his ailing close friend in Calcutta in 1940 whom he fondly called "Charlie". Who is he?

8. Gandhiji as a law student in London wearing the badge designed by him for

9. A great patriot and a pioneering radical nationalist, he died in 1920. On his death Gandhiji observed: "In the battle for freedom he gave no quarter and asked for none. For us he will go down to the generations yet unborn as a maker of modern India." Who is he?

10. Identify the lady helping Gandhiji to clean his feet after his evening walk.

11. A trusted associate of Gandhiji, he was elected President of the Indian National Congress at the age of only 35 years, the youngest to hold that office. After Independence and until his death in 1958, he served as Education Minister in Nehru's Cabinet. Identify him.

12. The person on the left of Gandhiji played a leading role in the sphere of eradication of untouchability and was one of the stalwarts of the Harijan Sewak Sangh. Who is he?

13. Identify the person in a smiling pose in the company of Gandhiji.

14. Which is this building where Gandhiji was detained during the Quit India Movement of 1942?

15. Gandhiji is seen here with his hand on the shoulder of a *dhoti*-clad follower and associate. Who is he?

16. The person on the left of Gandhiji, wearing spectacles, joined him as early as 1917 and served him faithfully till his death in 1942. Identify him.

17. A member of the Gandhi family, he played a leading role in organising the work of Gandhi Films Committee and was the editor of *The Hindustan Times*, New Delhi for quite many years. Who is he?

18. He was Gandhiji's official candidate for the Presidentship of the Indian National Congress at the Tripura session, but was defeated by Subhas Chandra Bose. Identify him.

19. He took a leading part in the welfare activities initiated by Gandhiji to improve the lot and status of Harijans in the country. He was the President of the All-India Depressed Classes League for ten years from 1936 and after Independence held important portfolios in the Central Government. Who is he?

20. Gandhiji alongwith another *satyagrahi* in South Africa in 1913. He was a German architect who joined Gandhiji's fold and became his close associate. Identify him.

21. Identify this prison where Gandhiji was lodged quite a few times during the thirties.

22. This is the famous woodcut of Gandhiji's Dandi March. Whose work is it?

23. Who is seen here with Gandhiji?

24. He came to be known to his contemporaries and to the succeeding generations of Indians as the 'Grand

Old Man of India'. He dedicated his entire life and wealth to the national movement. He was always ready to help and guide persons like Gandhiji who were engaged in the struggle for attaining *swaraj*. Who is he?

25. The person seen here with Gandhiji was appointed his successor to head the Salt March in the event of Gandhiji's arrest. Who is he?

26. A close associate of Gandhiji and a well-known author of many books on Gandhian themes, he was for some time the General Secretary of the Indian National Congress as also once its President. Identify him?

27. Besides being the Minister for Information and Broadcasting as also the Governor of Bihar, he was for some time the Chairman of the Gandhi National Memorial Trust and the Gandhi Peace Foundation. He also served as the Honorary Secretary of the National Committee for the Gandhi Centenary. Identify him.

28. Identify the person with Gandhiji wearing a Gandhi cap and a scarf. A great patriot and freedom fighter, he quit the Congress after being twice elected its President because of fundamental differences with Gandhiji both in respect of policy and tactics.

29. Gandhiji with the famous Congress leader from Bihar who later became the Chairman of the Constituent Assembly. Identify him.

30. Identify the lady on the right who was the resident medical attendant to Gandhiji and toured Noakhali with him during the communal riots in 1948.

31. In his effort to restore communal harmony in Delhi, Gandhiji paid a visit to this *dargah* at Mehrauli on January 27, 1948 just a couple of days before he was shot dead. Whose *dargah* is it?

32. An ardent admirer and a close associate of Gandhiji, he served as the Secretary, Gandhi Peace Foundation as also the Director of Gandhigram, Madurai. He brought out a number of works on Gandhian themes. Who is he?

33. Gandhiji is flanked on the extreme right by Brijkrishan Chandiwala. Who is on his extreme left?

34. Identify the well-known foreign dignitary with Gandhiji in 1942.

35. Gandhiji told the person seen with him towards the end of March, 1942: "Why did you come if this is what you have to offer? I advise you to take the first plane back home." Who is he?

1

2

3

4

5

6

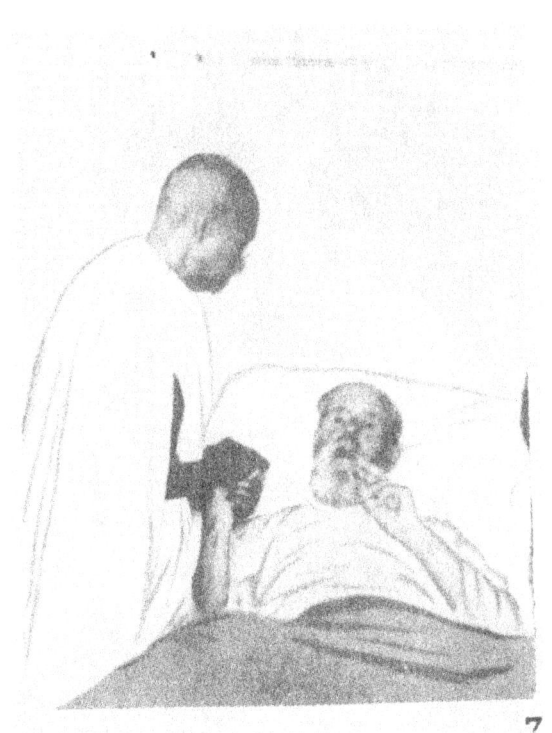

7

8

9

10

11

12

13

14

16

17

18

19

20

21

22

23

24

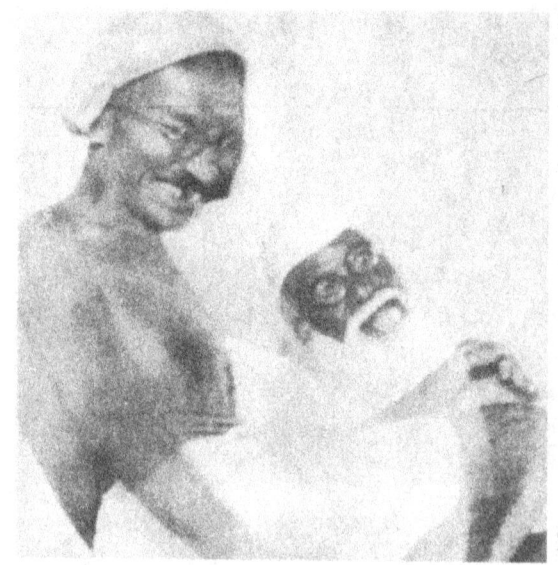

25

26

27

28

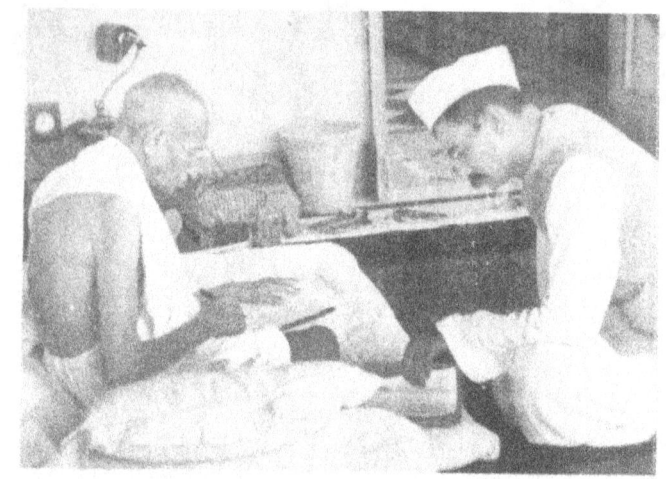

29

30

31

32

34

35

Answers

1. Family and Personal History

1. (c)	2. (a)	3. (d)	4. (b)	5. (d)
6. (b)	7. (d)	8. (c)	9. (d)	10. (a)
11. (c)	12. (d)	13. (b)	14. (a)	15. (c)
16. (a)	17. (d)	18. (b)	19. (c)	20. (d)
21. (b)	22. (b)	23. (a)	24. (c)	25. (c)
26. (c)	27. (d)	28. (a)	29. (a)	30. (d)
31. (c)	32. (b)	33. (a)	34. (b)	35. (d)
36. (d)	37. (b)	38. (b)	39. (c)	40. (d)
41. (c)	42. (b)	43. (d)	44. (a)	45. (b)
46. (c)	47. (c)	48. (d)	49. (a)	50. (c)
51. (b)	52. (d)	53. (c)	54. (a)	55. (a)
56. (d)	57. (b)	58. (d)	59. (b)	60. (c)
61. (d)	62. (c)	63. (b)	64. (a)	65. (c)
66. (c)	67. (b)	68. (c)	69. (a)	70. (b)
71. (d)	72. (b)	73. (a)	74. (d)	75. (b)
76. (d)	77. (c)	78. (a)	79. (d)	80. (a)
81. (b)	82. (a)	83. (c)	84. (c)	85. (d)
86. (c)	87. (a)	88. (b)	89. (a)	90. (d)
91. (c)	92. (a)	93. (d)	94. (d)	95. (a)
96. (b)				

2. South Africa Phase

1. (b)	2. (a)	3. (d)	4. (c)	5. (a)
6. (c)	7. (b)	8. (b)	9. (c)	10. (d)
11. (a)	12. (b)	13. (a)	14. (d)	15. (b)
16. (c)	17. (a)	18. (c)	19. (d)	20. (c)
21. (c)	22. (b)	23. (c)	24. (d)	25. (b)
26. (a)	27. (c)	28. (b)	29. (c)	30. (d)
31. (a)	32. (c)	33. (a)	34. (d)	35. (b)
36. (c)	37. (b)	38. (a)	39. (a)	40. (c)
41. (d)	42. (a)	43. (d)	44. (c)	45. (b)
46. (a)	47. (d)	48. (d)	49. (a)	50. (d)
51. (b)	52. (c)	53. (a)	54. (b)	55. (d)
56. (a)	57. (b)	58. (c)	59. (b)	60. (a)
61. (c)	62. (a)	63. (c)	64. (b)	65. (a)
66. (d)	67. (c)	68. (d)	69. (b)	70. (a)
71. (b)	72. (c)	73. (b)	74. (a)	75. (b)
76. (d)	77. (d)	78. (b)	79. (a)	80. (c)
81. (c)	82. (a)	83. (d)	84. (a)	85. (b)
86. (d)	87. (a)	88. (b)	89. (c)	90. (a)
91. (d)	92. (c)	93. (a)	94. (d)	95. (b)
96. (c)	97. (c)	98. (d)	99. (a)	100. (a)
101. (d)	102. (b)	103. (c)	104. (a)	105. (c)
106. (b)	107. (c)	108. (a)	109. (d)	110. (c)

3. Role in National Movement: Initial Phase

1. (a)	2. (b)	3. (c)	4. (d)	5. (c)
6. (b)	7. (b)	8. (a)	9. (d)	10. (c)
11. (b)	12. (b)	13. (d)	14. (a)	15. (c)
16. (b)	17. (a)	18. (c)	19. (a)	20. (b)

21. (d)	22. (c)	23. (d)	24. (b)	25. (c)
26. (a)	27. (b)	28. (d)	29. (a)	30. (c)
31. (b)	32. (c)	33. (a)	34. (d)	35. (b)
36. (c)	37. (d)	38. (a)	39. (a)	40. (b)
41. (c)	42. (d)	43. (b)	44. (a)	45. (b)
46. (d)	47. (b)	48. (a)	49. (c)	50. (a)
51. (b)	52. (d)	53. (a)	54. (d)	55. (b)
56. (c)	57. (a)	58. (b)	59. (d)	60. (b)
61. (a)	62. (c)	63. (d)	64. (a)	65. (c)
66. (d)	67. (a)	68. (b)	69. (b)	70. (b)
71. (c)	72. (b)	73. (a)	74. (c)	75. (d)
76. (c)	77. (d)	78. (c)	79. (d)	80. (b)
81. (a)	82. (b)	83. (c)	84. (d)	85. (a)
86. (b)	87. (a)	88. (c)	89. (d)	90. (b)
91. (d)	92. (a)	93. (b)	94. (c)	95. (d)
96. (b)	97. (a)	98. (a)		

4. Role in National Movement: Later Phase

1. (c)	2. (b)	3. (d)	4. (b)	5. (a)
6. (c)	7. (d)	8. (b)	9. (a)	10. (d)
11. (c)	12. (a)	13. (c)	14. (b)	15. (a)
16. (c)	17. (a)	18. (b)	19. (d)	20. (d)
21. (c)	22. (a)	23. (b)	24. (a)	25. (c)
26. (d)	27. (a-b)	28. (b)	29. (a)	30. (b)
31. (c)	32. (a)	33. (b)	34. (c)	35. (c)
36. (b)	37. (a)	38. (d)	39. (a)	40. (a)
41. (d)	42. (b)	43. (c)	44. (b)	45. (c)
46. (b)	47. (a)	48. (d)	49. (c)	50. (d)
51. (d)	52. (b)	53. (a)	54. (b)	55. (c)
56. (a)	57. (d)	58. (d)	59. (b)	60. (d)

61. (a)	62. (b)	63. (c)	64. (a)	65. (d)
66. (d)	67. (b)	68. (a)	69. (c)	70. (d)
71. (b)	72. (d)	73. (b)	74. (c)	75. (a)
76. (b)	77. (a)	78. (c)	79. (b)	80. (c)
81. (b)	82. (d)	83. (a)	84. (d)	85. (d)
86. (b)	87. (c)	88. (a)	89. (d)	90. (d)
91. (a)	92. (b)	93. (b)	94. (c)	95. (a)
96. (d)	97. (a)	98. (b)	99. (c)	100. (d)
101. (a)	102. (b)	103. (c)		

5. Thought and Philosophy

1. (a)	2. (b)	3. (d)	4. (c)	5. (d)
6. (c)	7. (a)	8. (b)	9. (c)	10. (d)
11. (b)	12. (c)	13. (a)	14. (b)	15. (b)
16. (a)	17. (b)	18. (d)	19. (a)	20. (c)
21. (d)	22. (a)	23. (a)	24. (c)	25. (d)
26. (c)	27. (d)	28. (a)	29. (a)	30. (b)
31. (c)	32. (a)	33. (c)	34. (a)	35. (d)
36. (a)	37. (d)	38. (b)	39. (d)	40. (c)
41. (b)	42. (c)	43. (a)	44. (b)	45. (a)
46. (d)	47. (d)	48. (d)	49. (a)	50. (b)
51. (a)	52. (d)	53. (b)	54. (c)	55. (d)
56. (b)	57. (d)	58. (d)	59. (a)	60. (a)
61. (c)	62. (a)	63. (b)	64. (d)	65. (c)
66. (d)	67. (a)	68. (b)	69. (a)	70. (b)
71. (c)	72. (b)	73. (c)	74. (d)	75. (a)
76. (d)	77. (b)	78. (c)	79. (c)	80. (b)
81. (d)	82. (b)	83. (d)	84. (b)	85. (a)
86. (c)	87. (d)	88. (c)	89. (b)	90. (c)
91. (a)	92. (d)	93. (c)		

6. Literature

1. (b)	2. (d)	3. (a)	4. (b)	5. (c)
6. (a)	7. (b)	8. (d)	9. (a)	10. (a)
11. (b)	12. (b)	13. (d)	14. (a)	15. (b)
16. (b)	17. (a)	18. (c)	19. (b)	20. (c)
21. (d)	22. (b)	23. (c)	24. (d)	25. (b)
26. (d)	27. (b)	28. (a)	29. (c)	30. (b)
31. (c)	32. (d)	33. (a)	34. (b)	35. (a)
36. (b)	37. (a)	38. (c)	39. (d)	40. (b)
41. (a)	42. (c)	43. (b)	44. (b)	45. (c)
46. (b)	47. (a)	48. (b)	49. (d)	50. (b)
51. (d)	52. (d)	53. (c)	54. (b)	55. (a)
56. (b)	57. (a)	58. (c)	59. (a)	60. (a)
61. (c)	62. (b)	63. (c)	64. (b)	65. (a)
66. (d)	67. (a)	68. (b)	69. (c)	70. (b)
71. (d)	72. (a)	73. (b)	74. (d)	75. (a)
76. (b)	77. (c)	78. (b)	79. (a)	80. (c)
81. (c)				

7. Associations and Institutions

1. (a)	2. (d)	3. (b)	4. (c)	5. (d)
6. (a)	7. (a)	8. (d)	9. (b)	10. (c)
11. (d)	12. (a)	13. (b)	14. (a)	15. (d)
16. (d)	17. (c)	18. (b)	19. (d)	20. (b)
21. (c)	22. (a)	23. (b)	24. (d)	25. (c)
26. (c)	27. (b)	28. (d)	29. (b)	30. (c)
31. (b)	32. (a)	33. (b)	34. (b)	35. (a)
36. (d)	37. (a)	38. (b)	39. (c)	40. (a)
41. (c)	42. (a)	43. (d)	44. (b)	45. (c)

46. (c)	47. (b)	48. (b)	49. (a)	50. (b)
51. (c)	52. (a)	53. (b)	54. (d)	55. (a)
56. (b)	57. (b)	58. (a)	59. (c)	60. (b)
61. (d)	62. (b)	63. (d)	64. (a)	65. (b)
66. (a)	67. (c)	68. (b)	69. (c)	70. (d)
71. (a)	72. (d)	73. (b)	74. (c)	75. (b)
76. (a)	77. (a)	78. (c)	79. (d)	80. (a)
81. (b)	82. (a)	83. (c)	84. (b)	85. (b)

8. Contemporaries

1. (a)	2. (c)	3. (b)	4. (a)	5. (b)
6. (c)	7. (d)	8. (b)	9. (c)	10. (a)
11. (d)	12. (d)	13. (a)	14. (c)	15. (b)
16. (a)	17. (b)	18. (d)	19. (c)	20. (b)
21. (c)	22. (c)	23. (d)	24. (b)	25. (d)
26. (c)	27. (b)	28. (c)	29. (c)	30. (b)
31. (a)	32. (a)	33. (a)	34. (b)	35. (c)
36. (a)	37. (b)	38. (a)	39. (c)	40. (b)
41. (a)	42. (c)	43. (a)	44. (d)	45. (b)
46. (c)	47. (b)	48. (d)	49. (a)	50. (d)
51. (b)	52. (a)	53. (b)	54. (c)	55. (d)
56. (c)	57. (b)	58. (a)	59. (b)	60. (c)
61. (b)	62. (a)	63. (b)	64. (a)	65. (b)
66. (c)	67. (d)	68. (d)	69. (d)	70. (c)
71. (a)	72. (a)	73. (b)	74. (c)	75. (a)
76. (d)	77. (b)	78. (c)	79. (a)	80. (d)
81. (d)	82. (d)	83. (b)	84. (c)	85. (b)

9. Photo Quiz

1. Gopal Krishna Gokhale
2. Motilal Nehru
3. Sarojini Naidu
4. Khan Abdul Ghaffar Khan
5. Sardar Vallabbhai Patel
6. Sevagram
7. C.F. Andrews
8. Vegetarian Society
9. Bal Gangadhar Tilak
10. Kasturbai Gandhi
11. Abul Kalam Azad
12. A.V. Thakkar
13. M.A. Jinnah
14. Aga Khan Palace
15. Vinoba Bhave
16. Mahadev Desai
17. Devdas Gandhi
18. S. Pattabhi Sitaramayya
19. Jagjivan Ram
20. Hermann Kallenbach
21. Verauda Jail
22. Nandlal Bose
23. Romain Rolland
24. Dadabhai Naoroji
25. Abbas Tyabji
26. J.B. Kripalani
27. R.R. Diwakar
28. Subhas Chandra Bose
29. Rajendra Prasad

30. Sushila Nayar
31. Bakhtiar Chiote
32. G. Ramachandran
33. Pyarelal
34. Marshal Chiang Kai-shek
35. Sir Stafford Cripps

www.ingramcontent.com/pod-product-compliance
Lightning Source LLC
Chambersburg PA
CBHW051342020726
47501CB00007B/2220